THE MOVIE BOYS IN THE JUNGLE

THE MOVIE BOYS SERIES LIST

THE MOVIE BOYS IN THE JUNGLE

THE MOVIE BOYS ON CALL, or *Filming the Perils of A Great City.*

THE MOVIE BOYS IN THE WILD WEST, or *Stirring Days Among the Cowboys and Indians.*

THE MOVIE BOYS AND THE WRECKERS, or *Facing the Perils of the Deep.*

THE MOVIE BOYS IN THE JUNGLE, or *Lively Times Among the Wild Beasts.*

THE MOVIE BOYS IN EARTHQUAKE LAND, or *Filming Pictures and Strange Perils.*

THE MOVIE BOYS AND THE FLOOD, or *Perilous Days on the Mighty Mississippi.*

THE MOVIE BOYS IN PERIL, or *Strenuous Days Along the Panama Canal.*

THE MOVIE BOYS UNDER THE SEA, or *The Treasure of the Lost Ship.*

THE MOVIE BOYS UNDER FIRE, or *The Search for the Stolen Film.*

THE MOVIE BOYS UNDER UNCLE SAM, or *Taking Pictures for the Army.*

THE MOVIE BOYS' FIRST SHOWHOUSE, or *Fighting for a Foothold in Fairlands.*

THE MOVIE BOYS AT SEASIDE PARK, or *The Rival Photo Houses of the Boardwalk.*

THE MOVIE BOYS ON BROADWAY, or *The Mystery of the Missing Cash Box.*

THE MOVIE BOYS' OUTDOOR EXHIBITION, or *The Film that Solved the Mystery.*

THE MOVIE BOYS' NEW IDEA, or *Getting the Best of Their Enemies.*

THE MOVIE BOYS AT THE BIG FAIR, or *The Greatest Film Ever Exhibited.*

THE MOVIE BOYS' WAR SPECTACLE, or *The Film that Won the Prize.*

THE MOVIE BOYS IN THE JUNGLE

VICTOR APPLETON

Originally published in 1913.

Published by Wildside Press .

Visit us online at wildsidepress.com.

INTRODUCTION
KARL WURF

The Movie Boys in the Jungle is part of a lesser-known but fascinating Stratemeyer Syndicate series issued under the Victor Appleton name. First appearing in the 1910s, the Movie Boys stories followed Joe Duncan and Blake Stewart, two adventurous young cameramen whose exploits took them from the American West to Africa, Asia, and beyond. The first five volumes of the series were re-printed as the last five volumes of the Moving Picture Boys series. In turn, both the Motion Picture Chums and Moving Picture Boys were combined in 1926 as the Movie Boys series. The text for this volume was taken from the 1926 reissue.

The Movie Boys series reflected the cultural excitement surrounding early motion pictures, which were then a new and rapidly evolving technology. The tales blended adventure fiction with practical details about filmmaking, giving readers both thrills and an introduction to how cameras and films worked.

The series came from the Stratemeyer Syndicate, a pioneering book-packaging firm created by Edward Stratemeyer. Stratemeyer rarely wrote the books himself. Instead, he plotted the stories, assigned them to anonymous writers (paid a flat fee), and published them under "house names" such as Victor Appleton, Roy Rockwood, Laura Lee Hope, and Franklin W. Dixon. This system produced some of the most successful juvenile series of the twentieth century.

Although *The Movie Boys* never achieved the lasting popularity of other Stratemeyer properties, the series helped pave the way for more successful brands. For instance, under the same Victor Appleton byline came *Tom Swift*, the wildly popular inventor-hero whose stories ran for decades. Other Syndicate hits included *The Hardy Boys* (Franklin W. Dixon), *Nancy Drew* (Carolyn Keene), *The Bobbsey Twins* (Laura Lee Hope), *Bomba the Jungle Boy* (Roy Rockwood), and *The Rover Boys* (Arthur M. Winfield, a pseudonym used by Stratemeyer himself). These series dominated the children's adventure market for much of the twentieth century, setting formulas still echoed in popular fiction today.

Edward Stratemeyer (1862–1930) was one of the most influential figures in American popular publishing. By systematizing series production, he created a virtual factory of children's literature that shaped the reading habits of millions. His model emphasized fast-paced adventure, recurring heroes, and cliffhanger plotting, all designed to keep readers coming back for the next volume. Even after his death, his daughters Harriet Stratemeyer Adams and Edna Stratemeyer Squier continued the Syndicate's work, ensuring the survival of Nancy Drew, the Hardy Boys, and others well into the late twentieth century.

Seen in this light, *The Movie Boys in the Jungle* is more than a single juvenile adventure story. It is part of a larger publishing experiment that bridged the dime novel era and modern series fiction, reflecting both America's fascination with exotic adventure and its enthusiasm for the then-new magic of motion pictures.

CHAPTER I
UNEXPECTED NEWS

"THAT'S THE WAY TO do it! Jump right into the surf and get after her, Mr. Piper!"

"Move a little faster, can't you?"

"If he doesn't that big wave is going to get him as sure as fate!"

"There he goes! Stop those moving picture machines, boys!"

A big wave came tumbling up the beach, rolling over and over in its foamy grip a man clad in a life guard's bathing costume; while farther up the sands two lads, at the handles of moving picture cameras, ceased grinding away at the film, and doubled up with mirth.

Then, when the wave had spent its force, the man arose, got rid of the water in his eyes and the sand in his mouth, and exclaimed:

"I knew it! I knew something would happen if you tried one of these light-house dramas! I'm done! I quit here and now!"

"Oh, C. C., just one more trial!" pleaded a man who seemed to be a theatrical manager. "You can do it if you try again; I'm sure you can!"

"Never again!" cried the man, and then the two boys and the other members of the company gathered about him to use their persuasion.

"C. C. is up to his old tricks; isn't he, Blake?" remarked one of the lads, as he looked at his moving picture machine to see how many feet of film had been registered.

"That's what he is, Joe," responded the other youth. "But I don't know as I can blame him this time. Something did happen, in spite of the fact that he's always predicting calamities that seldom come to pass."

"Think they'll get him to try it again?"

"Oh, yes, I guess so. Mr. Ringold and Mr. Hadley generally get what they want. There, he's going to do it over again. I guess we'd better get back to our machines," for the lads had joined the group about the man in bathing costume.

"Well, I'll try that rescue scene once more," finally announced the person who had been designated as Mr. Piper and also as C. C.

"But it does seem," he went on, "that I always have to do all the work in these tank dramas. I'm the one that's always falling in the water and getting my death of cold. I always have to do the rescuing. Why can't I be rescued myself some time? Though I suppose if I jumped in, and waited for some one to get me out, they'd let me drown. Oh, why did I ever go into this miserable business, anyhow?" and while uttering these dismal words the man made a series of comical faces that sent the others into spasms of laughter.

"Oh, cheer up, Gloomy!" cried one of the young ladies of the company. "You'll be happy yet."

"I doubt it," came the answer. "But go ahead!"

"All ready out there!" called Mr. Ringold, head of the Film Theatrical Company, which was making a series of dramas for moving pictures on the lower California coast, near San Diego. "All ready out there in the boat! C. C. is going to try the rescue once more."

"And look out for the big waves, C. C.," advised the manager. "Just swim as you always do. You've been in the surf before. And you're supposed to be a life guard, you know. They can swim like fishes."

"I'm not a fish!" declared the actor.

"Be ready, Miss Lee!" called Mr. Ringold, to a young lady, who was out some distance on the lazily rising and falling ocean, in a small boat. "Remember you're supposed to be adrift in an open craft—you have been lost for days and days. You finally get near shore and the life guard sees you. He swims out at the peril of his life and rescues you."

"That's it—always at the risk of my life," grumbled C. C. Piper, to give him his right name. "If I don't drown, I get my death of cold!"

"Go ahead!" cried Mr. Ringold, impatiently. "Remember, Miss Lee, you're supposed to be nearly starved. The life guard brings you in and carries you to the lighthouse. There you fall in love with the young keeper, and the life guard and he have trouble over you. But we'll get those scenes later. All ready now, C. C. Jump in. Joe—Blake, be ready with your cameras there!"

"All right!" cried the two lads, and, as the actor once more plunged into the surf, Joe and Blake began turning the handles of the moving picture cameras.

The machines clicked and purred as the film unwound from one reel, passed behind the lens with its rapidly opening and closing shutter, and then was wound on another reel, pictures being taken at the rate of sixteen per second.

This time nothing happened. C. C. swam out to the boat containing Miss Lee, one of the younger actresses, brought her to shore, and she was carried into the lighthouse, which was near at hand.

"That'll be all for the present, boys," directed Mr. Ringold. "The next scenes will take place in the lighthouse, and I'll have to arrange for some lights there, as it's too dark to get the pictures without. I won't need you for several hours, and then this will bring our work on the Pacific coast to a close."

"That lets us out, Blake," said one lad to the other. "What shall we do?"

"Go back to the boarding house and finish packing up, I guess. If we're going to make that trip to China, to look for your sister, who is supposed to be with some missionaries there, we've got lots to do yet. Where is your father?"

"He went to the postoffice to see if there was any mail. He expected something from that missionary to whom he wrote for more explicit directions how to get to the station where my sister Jessie is supposed to be. He had rather indefinite ones when he started for Hong Kong, just before he was wrecked."

"That's so. I say, Joe! It's going to be quite an experience for us to go to China. I'm glad you thought of taking a moving picture camera along. We will get some good films, I believe."

"So do I, but I won't be much interested in them until I find my sister."

"I suppose not. Well, come on back to our shack," and the two lads, Joe Duncan and Blake Stewart, moving picture operators, who had been engaged to "film" a series of dramas on the Pacific coast for Mr. Ringold, packed up their machines and left the beach. The theatrical company went inside the government lighthouse, which they had been permitted to use for part of the moving picture play.

Some months before, Joe and Blake, after a series of strange adventures, which I shall tell you about in brief, presently, reached San Diego with the company. Joe was on the track of his father, whom he had not seen since he was a baby. He learned that Mr. Duncan was an assistant keeper at the very lighthouse in which the little drama was now taking place.

But Mr. Duncan had left there just before Joe and his chum, Blake, arrived. It was said he had fled to escape being arrested as a wrecker of ships by means of false lights, but this was disproved, and it was learned that Mr. Duncan had set out for China to find his daughter Jessie, who had disappeared at the same time as had Joe.

But the vessel on which Mr. Duncan sailed was wrecked. He was picked up by a ship bound for San Francisco, and this craft foundered, too, in a great storm near San Diego.

It chanced that Mr. Ringold wanted moving pictures of a storm and a wreck, and while the life savers were rigging up the breeches buoy to bring ashore the unfortunates, Joe and Blake took moving pictures of the stirring scene.

The last to come ashore was the captain and Mr. Duncan, and thus Joe found his father. The latter cleared himself of the false charge, and told how he had been seeking his daughter, who was said to be a missionary's helper in China.

Of course, Joe at once decided to give up his work for the Film Theatrical Company and accompany his parent on the quest, and Blake elected to go with his boyhood chum. But there were a few moving pictures yet to be taken to finish the work on the coast, and the boys agreed to do them for Mr. Ringold. This was what they were engaged on when the present story opens.

"I wonder what it will be like in China?" mused Joe, as he and his chum walked on.

"Oh, just like what we've read about, I expect. Men with pigtails, and women with fans, tea gardens, vases, dragons, and all that."

"We ought to get some pretty good pictures, then," went on Joe.

"That's right," agreed Blake.

"I can hardly wait to start," continued his chum. "To think that I've found my father, when I never expected to see him again, and that I'm going to have a sister. I'll soon have quite a family, Blake."

"That's what you will. Well, I wish you luck. I wonder what your sister Jessie will be like?"

"She's about a year older than I am," remarked Joe. "Dad said so. And he said she was very pretty when she was a baby. Poor Jessie! To think that she doesn't know she has a father any more than I did a few months ago. Won't she be surprised when we come walking in on her, over in China, and ask for a cup of tea?"

"I guess she will, Joe. Well, I'm going to pack up. We have only about a week more here, and then Ho! for Hong Kong!"

"That's right. Say, I'll need two trunks to take all the truck I've accumulated since we came here."

"You'll have to leave some of it, I reckon."

For a time there was silence in the rooms of the two lads, broken only by the noise they made in packing their trunks. Presently Joe said:

"Seems to me Dad is a long while coming back from the postoffice," for Mr. Duncan had taken up his residence with his son in the big theatrical boarding house on the beach.

"It's quite a walk into town," observed Blake.

"I'll tell you what let's do," suggested his chum.

"What?"

"Let's walk in and meet him. Then I'll know sooner just where my sister is. I want to write to her."

"All right, I'm with you; come on," and the two, leaving their packing half finished, started for San Diego, which was some miles from the little fishing settlement of Chester, where most of the films had been made.

"That looks like him coming," observed Blake, some time afterward, when he and his chum had walked on for a considerable distance toward the town. "It walks like him, anyhow."

"Yes, that's Dad," observed Joe. "Say, do you know he's just like I pictured him in my mind, after we met Uncle Bill, the time he rescued us from those Moqui Indians. Dad is just as I thought he'd be; a bit younger, perhaps, but otherwise the same."

"That's good. It's nice not to be disappointed. But he seems to have a letter, Joe."

"That's right; he has. I hope it's from Jessie, though that can hardly be, as Dad only wrote to the missionary headquarters in New York to find out her exact location in China. But he sure has something," and Joe looked closely at the man who was approaching, holding in his hand a bit of paper.

At that moment Mr. Duncan looked up and saw his son and the latter's chum. But he did not quicken his pace, though Joe broke into a run.

"Hello, Dad!" he cried. "Any news?"

"Yes—there—there's some news, Joe," was the answer.

"That's rather odd," mused Blake. "He doesn't speak as if it was good news. I wonder if anything could have happened?"

The same thought must have come to Joe, for he hesitated a moment, and then, hastening on, was soon at his father's side.

"What's the matter, Dad?" he exclaimed. "Is anything wrong? Isn't Jessie in China? Is she—is she dead?"

"No, Joe, not dead, as far as I can make out, but I have unexpected news just the same—news I don't like!" and he looked at the letter in his hand.

"What is it, Dad? Tell me!" urged his son. "Has anything happened to Jessie? Isn't she in China?"

"No, Joe, she isn't."

"Where is she?"

"Why, this letter from the missionary society says she changed her mind at the last minute, and instead of going to China went to the interior of Africa."

"To Africa!" cried Joe.

"Yes, into the jungle; and Joe," went on Mr. Duncan, with a tremor in his voice, "it's in a locality where the natives are said to be none too friendly. Poor Jessie! My poor little girl!" and Mr. Duncan turned his face away.

CHAPTER II
ON TO NEW YORK

JOE DUNCAN LOOKED AT his chum Blake Stewart in surprise. Neither knew what to say, and Mr. Duncan seemed so affected by the unexpected news that his son was seriously alarmed.

But Joe was used to meeting emergencies. His work in taking moving pictures had put him in good trim for this. In a moment he had recovered his poise.

"Gone to Africa; eh?" he exclaimed. "Well, I don't know that Africa is much farther than China, Dad," and he spoke cheerfully.

"What do you mean, son?"

"I mean that if Jessie has gone to Africa we'll go there to get her!"

"That's it!" cried Blake. "The jungles of Africa can't be much worse than the wild parts of China."

"But the natives!" exclaimed Mr. Duncan. "This letter says that the African tribes are on the verge of an uprising. If that had been known before Jessie started they would not have let her go. As it is, they have written to her, and the missionaries she is with—a man and his wife—to come back. But it will be some time before they get the letter, for they are far in the interior."

"Well, don't worry, Dad," advised Joe, cheerfully. "We'll make out all right. We'll soon start after her and get her away from those natives—if they chance to have her."

"Do you mean that?" cried Mr. Duncan.

"I sure do, Dad. The jungles of Africa, or the wilds of China—it's all the same to us; isn't it, Blake?"

"It sure is. Count me in!"

"And will you come with us?" asked Joe's father.

"I certainly will!" came the quick answer.

"And we won't lose any time," added Joe. "We were going to engage passage to China; it will be just as easy to do so to Africa, though it may take a little longer. Now let's get back to the boarding house and arrange the details."

And, while father and son, with the latter's chum, are on their way back to the fishing hamlet, I will take the opportunity to make my new readers a little better acquainted with Joe and Blake—the moving picture boys—whose adventures they are soon to follow in the "Dark Continent."

The lads were first told of in the initial volume of this series, entitled "The Movie Boys on Call"; or "Filming the Perils of a great City." In the beginning Blake Stewart worked for his uncle, Jonathan Haverstraw, in the village of Fayetteburg, in the middle part of New York State. Mr. Haverstraw had a farm, and on an adjoining one, owned by Zachariah Bradley, Joe Duncan worked. Joe thought himself without relatives, since from his earliest days he could remember none.

Owing to the fact that Mr. Bradley found he could no longer pay Joe's wages, and because Blake's uncle decided to give up his farm and retire to a home for the aged, the two lads unexpectedly found themselves without positions at the same time, Blake having no other relative than Mr. Haverstraw.

But, just at this time, a Mr. Calvert Hadley came to Fayetteburg with a theatrical company to take some moving pictures. The boys met him, and after some negotiations were engaged by him to go to New York.

There they learned the business and helped Mr. Hadley, who was engaged in getting out a "moving picture newspaper," showing the perils of the great city, odd scenes and happenings, train wrecks, burning buildings and the like. The boys liked the work very much, though often they were in great danger. They managed to cause the arrest of a reckless autoist who had smashed the carriage of Mrs. Betty Randolph, a Southern lady living in Fayetteburg, and, securing the reward she had offered, Blake and Joe bought moving picture cameras for themselves. Then they went into business on their own account, making all sorts of films to order.

It was while engaged in this work that a strange commission came to them. The second volume of the series, called "The Movie Boys in the Wild West"; or "Stirring Days Among the Cowboys and Indians," tells of this in detail.

In brief, the boys one day learned that a number of the Moqui and Navajo Indians had left their reservations in Arizona, and had hidden themselves in the desert, there to go through some of their ancient dances and ceremonies.

A certain geographical society was anxious to get a series of films of these ceremonies, and offered a prize for the best ones. Joe and Blake decided to try for it, as did a number of other concerns, including one that was a rival of our heroes.

Before leaving for the West, however, Joe received a strange letter. It intimated that he might find his father, of whose existence he was uncertain. The letter was written by a roving cowboy, and the only clue was that he had been at Big B ranch somewhere in Arizona. He forgot to mention just where.

Full of hope, not only of getting films of the Indians, but of finding Mr. Duncan, Joe and Blake started out. They had many adventures, for the theatrical company went with them, Mr. Ringold, the proprietor, needing some films of the West, with cowboys and Indians. After "filming" a number of Western dramas, Joe and Blake started off to find the hidden Indians. Unexpectedly they located Big B ranch, but the cowboy who had written the letter was gone. However, another cowboy, Hank Selby by name, decided to go with the lads to help find the Indians, for Joe and Blake were tenderfeet.

They located the fanatical Moquis, got the films of the weird dances, were attacked and saved, not only themselves, but their rivals. Joe's uncle, Bill Duncan, chanced to be one of the United States troopers who drove the Indians back to their reservation.

Joe's uncle gave news of Joe's father. The latter, it seems, had been made a widower when the two children—Joe and Jessie—were young. He placed them in the care of a family, and went to the gold fields. When he came back—quite a rich man—the two children had disappeared and he could find no trace of them, as the family he left them with had separated.

Joe's uncle said the lad's father was a lighthouse keeper somewhere on the California coast, and, after the Indian pictures had been obtained, Joe decided to look for his parent. Blake offered to accompany him.

The boys thought they would have to say good-bye to their theatrical friends, but Mr. Ringold had long contemplated a series of sea dramas, and, learning that the two lads were going to the coast, he hired them, together with Mr. Hadley, to make the films near the Pacific Ocean.

In the third book of the series, entitled "The Movie Boys and the Wreckers"; or "Facing the Perils of the Deep," you will find the details of further strange happenings.

Mr. Duncan, so Joe learned, was assistant keeper of a lighthouse near San Diego. Going there with the company, which engaged quarters in the beach settlement of Chester, Joe sought his parent. But, to his surprise, Mr. Duncan had left unexpectedly, and the lightkeeper intimated to Blake, privately, that it was a good thing he had.

Pressed for a reason, the keeper said that detectives had come to arrest Mr. Duncan on a charge of having helped to wreck some vessels by means of false lights on the coast.

How the boys traced the real wreckers and assisted in their capture; how they took part in thrilling sea scenes, and helped make films for the theatrical company, I have set down fully in the book.

Then came the big storm, the wreck of the ship and the saving of the crew. Mr. Duncan was among them, and on the beach his son found him. The two were happy, and Mr. Duncan told of his long search for his children. He had given up hope of ever finding Joe, and was on his way to China to recover his daughter, of whom he had unexpectedly gotten trace, when he was wrecked. Then, after his rescue, he and Joe and Blake decided they would make a further attempt to reach the Flowery Kingdom.

Just a word about the theatrical company. There were the usual number of characters, but the one who caused the most amusement was Mr. Christopher Cutler Piper, who was variously called "C. C.," or "Gloomy." The reason for the latter nickname was that he was always predicting direful happenings which never came to pass, or was always looking on the dark side of things. And this in spite of the fact that he was supposed to be the comedian of the company, when not filling other rôles.

The reason he was called C. C. was because he did not like the name Christopher Cutler. He said the boys used to call him "Christopher Custard," so he used his initials only, and asked others to do the same. He was a source of much amusement to his friends, including the boys.

"And so we are to go to Africa instead of China," remarked Blake, when he and his chum, with Mr. Duncan, had reached the boarding house.

"So it seems," spoke Joe. "Just in what part of Africa is Jessie, Dad? Jove! how queer it seems to be using her name just as if I had known her all my life, when, as a matter of fact, I can't remember her."

"Why, as nearly as the society in New York can tell," answered Mr. Duncan, "she is with a Mr. and Mrs. Brown, at a missionary station somewhere near Entebbe, on the upper Victoria Nyanza. It's in the jungle, far from a white settlement. My poor little girl!"

"Don't worry, Dad! We'll find her!" exclaimed Joe.

"Of course we will!" said Blake, with a confidence he did not altogether feel. "I wish we were there now. I've always wanted to go to Africa."

"We'll have to start from New York," said Mr. Duncan, who had been looking at maps and steamer routes. "And the sooner we get there the better."

"We might as well travel with the theatrical crowd," suggested Blake. "They'll soon be leaving, and we'll have company. Besides, Mr. Ringold might decide to get some jungle dramas, and we could film them."

But the theatrical manager had no such intention.

"I'm going to run a series of city dramas," he said, when the boys told him the news. "Of course, I'd like to have you make the pictures for me, but if you are going to Africa you can't. However, Mr. Hadley will do it, and when you come back I may have a new commission for you. I wish you all sorts of luck."

"They'll never come back alive," predicted C. C., in his most gloomy tones, and then he continued to hum a comic song.

"Oh, don't be so melancholy," said Miss Lee, one of the actresses.

"Terrible place—African jungle," went on the comedian. "Fevers, wild animals, wilder natives, snakes, elephants, bugs of all kinds, swamps—ugh! Excuse me!"

"Oh, I guess we can manage," said Joe, cheerfully.

"If we can't we'll send for you," added Blake, with a laugh.

"Never!" cried C. C. Piper.

The final scenes at the lighthouse were filmed, the boys and their friends packed up, and then, accompanied by the theatrical company, Joe, Blake and Mr. Duncan started for New York, soon to embark for the jungles of Africa.

CHAPTER III
THE CIRCUS WRECK

"WE'RE MAKING GOOD TIME, Blake."

"That's right, Joe. It's a little too fast to suit me. I always get to thinking what would happen if we hit anything at full speed," and Blake Stewart looked out of the window rather apprehensively at the landscape flitting past.

"Oh, don't come any of that C. C. Piper talk," urged Joe, with a laugh at his chum. "Where is he, anyhow?"

"Up in the smoker, I fancy. He said he was going there."

"And he'll come back, and complain that he's full of tobacco germs, or something like that, and won't live a week."

"That's right," agreed Blake.

The boys, with Mr. Duncan and the theatrical company, were speeding East in a fast train, all of them anxious to reach New York. It was their second day since leaving the coast, and to Joe, though the train was making exceptionally fast time, as Blake remarked, the cars seemed fairly to crawl along.

"I suppose you're anxious to get there," remarked Blake, when they had stopped at a station, and were again on the move.

"Yes, they can't reach New York any too soon for us; can they, Dad?" and Joe glanced toward his father, who was looking at some papers.

"That's right, son," came the answer. "Every time I think of poor little Jessie, out there among those savages, it makes me nervous. I haven't seen her since she was a baby, when I left her in the care of the family I supposed would keep her until I could get back."

"What did they do with her?" asked Blake, who had not heard all the particulars.

"Well, they had bad luck, too, it seems, and had to separate. In that way both Joe and Jessie became lost to me, but I have Joe back," and he glanced fondly at his son.

"And you're not going to lose me again in a hurry, either!" exclaimed the lad. "Folks are too scarce with me to get rid of 'em when I don't have to. But, Dad, do you really think there is any danger for Jessie?"

"I don't know, son. I've been watching the newspapers lately, and they haven't said anything about trouble with the natives in Africa. Though it's so far off, and news travels so slowly in the jungle, that anything might have happened and we wouldn't know of it until it was all over."

"Oh, I wouldn't worry," suggested Blake. "She is in good hands; isn't she?"

"Yes, the head of the missionary society writes that Mr. and Mrs. Brown have had much experience in Africa. They know the natives, and the latter trust them. Jessie went as a sort of assistant to Mrs. Brown, you know. I can't imagine, though, why she should go into foreign work."

"Maybe she wanted to find you, Dad," suggested Joe. "You know one reason I came out to film those crazy Indians was to have a chance to look you up. Maybe Jessie did the same thing."

"Perhaps," admitted Mr. Duncan. "Well, I only hope she is all right. It will be some time before we can see her, even if we have good luck."

"What route are we going to take?" asked Blake, who was always interested in geography.

"From New York," spoke Mr. Duncan, consulting some memoranda he had made, "we take a German steamer for Naples, Italy."

"Italy!" cried Joe. "I thought we were going to Africa."

"We are," said his father; "but unless you want to land on the West coast, and travel all the way across the continent, which is almost impossible, in order to get to the Victoria Nyanza, the practical route is by way of Naples, the Mediterranean Sea, Suez Canal, Red Sea, Gulf of Aden, and so out into the Indian Ocean. We will land at Mombasa, and after a trip on the Uganda Railroad we will strike into the interior."

"It's a long trip," sighed Joe.

"Oh, we'll soon make it," spoke his father. "It's better than going around by way of the Cape of Good Hope, and striking up through the Mozambique channel between Africa and Madagascar. It won't take long, once we get to New York. But the journey in Africa, after we leave the railroad, may be tedious, and, I may as well add, not a little dangerous."

"Dangerous!" cried Joe.

"Yes, from wild men and wild beasts. But I am going to take all the precautions I can. I am, as you know, boys, fairly well off now, and I can afford to hire something of an expedition to help us in this quest after Jessie. We will have a safari and—"

"What's a safari?" asked Blake.

"It's what they call an expedition in Africa," explained Mr. Duncan. "It consists of porters and native policemen. It's the only way to travel. Of course, we won't have as large a one as certain well-known hunters have had, but we will do the best we can. I am bound to find my daughter if I spend my last cent!"

"And we're with you!" cried Blake. "You can have all my share of the business, Joe!" and he held out his hand to his chum.

"Thanks, old man!" replied the other, and moisture came to his eyes. "It's good of you, but I don't want to take your share of the profits."

"Of course you will!" cried Blake. "Didn't we make it together? And we'll spend it together!"

I might explain that the boys had done very well in their moving picture business, and the prize they won for the Indian films had given them a substantial bank account. Mr. Ringold also paid them well, and, though their expenses were heavy, they were fairly well off for boys.

"I don't believe we'll have to call on you, Blake," said Mr. Duncan, with a smile; "but I'm just as much obliged. If my funds do run out, I'll let you assist me, though, for I know you'll be glad to do it."

"That's what I will!" cried the lad. "I haven't many folks myself—only my aged uncle—but I want Joe to get all the relatives he can."

"And I'll share 'em with you," added his chum.

The train rushed on, seeming to increase in speed, and others than Blake looked apprehensively out of the windows as the landscape seemed fairly to fly past.

"What's the hurry, conductor?" asked Mr. Hadley, when that official came through, as the cars swept around a curve with such force that several held on to their seats in fear.

"Making up lost time," was the short response. "Don't get nervous. This is the best stretch of the whole road here."

"Then there's sure to be a wreck," predicted C. C. "It's always on the best stretches that the accidents occur. We'll leave the track, roll over in a ditch, or go through a bridge—I'm sure of it!"

"Oh, you horrid thing!" cried Miss Shay, another of the actresses. "Can't some of you men do something to him?" and she appealed to the actors of the company.

"We'll drop him at the next tank station, if he doesn't cut out that line of talk," declared Mr. Levinberg, who played the "villain."

"What! And have me starve to death?" cried Mr. Piper. "I had almost rather be wrecked in some nice locality where there was plenty to eat. A wreck there—"

He did not finish his words, for at that moment there came a grinding of the brakes on the wheels, so suddenly that several of the passengers were thrown from their seats.

"It's a wreck, all right!" yelled Blake, getting to his feet.

"Hold on, everybody!" cried Joe.

The train shook and trembled as the engineer endeavored, by the use of the emergency air brake, to bring it to a stop. Then there came a crash, a splintering of wood and a clang of metal.

It was followed by a curious combination of sounds. There were grunts, roars, squeals and trumpetings—the neighing of horses, and the shouts of men. Chains clanked, and a rumble, as of thunder, was heard.

Then the train came to a stop with a jolt that further shook up the theatrical company, which was traveling in a private car.

"For cats' sake—what's happened?" cried Blake.

"Some sort of a smash!" declared Joe, crawling out from under a seat, where he had been thrown.

Women were screaming, men were yelling and shouting. The hissing of escaping steam could be heard, and the moving picture boys, looking toward the forward end of their car, saw that part of the roof was torn off. But otherwise the vehicle was not much damaged, and no one appeared to be hurt save for minor cuts and bruises.

Suddenly Miss Lee, who had slid along the aisle to the front end, uttered a scream and came running back.

"What is it; are you hurt?" asked Blake, catching her as she was about to fall.

"No! No! I'm not hurt! But look! A snake! A snake is coming into the car! Oh, stop it!"

The boys looked to where she pointed. Through the crack in the roof something long and sinuous was thrust inside, and began feeling about. It was a dull slate color.

"Snake!" cried Joe. "That's no snake!"

"What is it, then?" demanded Blake.

"It's a trunk—an elephant's trunk!"

"An elephant!" screamed Miss Lee.

"Yes, we—"

"Then we've wrecked a circus train!" cried Blake. He put Miss Lee in a seat, and looked out of the window. "That's what's happened!" he yelled. "We've run into a circus train, and the wild animals are all over the track—most of 'em alive, too!"

CHAPTER IV
A GREAT OPPORTUNITY

BLAKE'S RINGING WORDS CAUSED no little excitement in the car—excitement that was already intense, owing to the crash of the wreck.

"What's that you said?" cried Mr. Duncan, for there was so much confusion that Blake's words did not carry clearly.

"We've struck a circus train," replied the boy. "Not a bad smash, I guess, for I don't see many cars piled up. But a lot of the animals are out."

"I knew it!" cried C. C. Piper. "I knew something would happen! If I don't drown I'm saved to be eaten by a lion! Oh, why did I ever go into this business?"

"Is there any danger, Blake?" cried Mr. Duncan, coming to the side of his son's chum, as Blake was looking out of the window. "Can you see if anyone is hurt?"

"No—none, though some of the animals seem to be killed. Joe, come on out and—"

He was interrupted by a roar, unmistakably that of a lion.

"Oh!" screamed Miss Lee. "That's a jungle beast, sure! Even though it wasn't a snake I saw, that's a lion."

"Yes, it's a lion," said Blake, withdrawing his head from the window; "but it's in a cage. They're running it off one of the smashed flat cars. The lion can't get out, Miss Lee."

"Thank goodness for that!" she exclaimed. "Oh, I'm so frightened."

The chorus of uncouth sounds kept up, but seemed to be lessening. Those in the car picked themselves up from the places whither they had been tossed. No one seemed to be much hurt, though C. C. was wiping blood from a cut on his hand.

"It's all right!" cried a brakeman, entering the private car at that moment. "It wasn't a bad crash. None of the passengers is killed."

"Are the lions and tigers loose?" asked Miss Shay.

"I—I guess not," said the brakeman, but the boys noticed that he appeared ill at ease. "You're to stay in here," he added. "We may bring some other passengers in here, as one of our cars is badly smashed."

"Bring 'em all in!" exclaimed Mr. Ringold. "There's plenty of room, and I'm something of a doctor. We've got a first-aid kit here."

"All right—thanks," spoke the brakeman, as he hurried out, and Blake noticed that he took care to shut the door after him. To the boy this meant something.

Blake looked toward the crack in the roof, through which the elephant had thrust its trunk. The big beast was no longer in evidence. Miss Lee, too, glanced nervously in the same direction. Blake had a sudden inspiration.

"Joe!" he exclaimed, in a whisper, when he saw that there was no need for their assistance in the theatrical car. "I've got a dandy scheme."

"What is it?"

"Let's film this wreck."

"Film it?" asked Joe, who seemed somewhat dazed from the shock of the accident.

"Yes, it will make some dandy moving pictures. A wrecked circus train, with some of the animals loose—the men trying to catch them—come on, let's get some views. One of our machines is in this car."

"That's right—I wish we had all three of them here," for the lads owned three—two worked by hand, and one an automatic, operated by a portable compressed air motor. But this, as well as one of the hand machines, was with their baggage sent on ahead.

"Come on!" cried Blake. "No time to lose. They'll get the beasts back in their cages as soon as they can."

"That's so," agreed his chum. "But if there are lions and tigers loose, Blake—"

"I don't believe there are," spoke Blake, quickly. "I didn't see any when I looked; but, if there are, the beasts will be too dazed to make any trouble. Come on."

"I'm with you!" cried Joe, and they got out their camera.

"What are you going to do?" asked Mr. Ringold, who was binding up a cut on Miss Shay's arm.

"Get some moving pictures of this."

"Good for you!" the theatrical manager cried. "Maybe I can work 'em in some of my dramas."

Joe and Blake were soon outside the car. A scene of confusion met their eyes, but it was not as bad as they had anticipated. The collision was what is known as a "side-swipe"—that is, the circus train stood on a siding, but not far enough beyond the switch, when the passenger train rushed by it and hit the other a glancing blow.

As it was, the passenger engine was damaged, as was the first car, and the next one—that on which our friends were. But the jar to the circus train had thrown some of the cages off the flat cars and broken them. Also a box car, containing a number of the elephants, had been smashed, as well as one containing some camels. A few of the animals had been killed.

"Lively work!" cried Blake, as he and his chum took in the scene.

"Yes, they're trying to catch 'em all," agreed Joe. "Set the camera here," and he indicated a piece of elevated ground.

The circus men were rushing here and there, under the directions of some-one who was evidently the manager. Sacred cows, crooked-neck camels and some ponies were being caught and driven back into one of the undam-aged cars. The elephants were seemingly the easiest to handle, though they showed a disposition to wander.

"Drive 'em over this way!" yelled the circus man. "I'll have heavy damages out of this railroad company, or my name isn't Harry Stone. The idea of smashing my outfit this way! Hi there! Don't let that pony get away! It's one of our best trick performers. Lasso him, if you have to!"

The circus men rushed up to an elephant that was about to take a stroll across the tracks and off into the open country. By hard work they succeeded in turning him back. A camel showed signs of fight, but was subdued.

Joe and Blake were getting a fine lot of films, but they had to work quickly, for the circus men, with the speed that is characteristic of them, were rapidly getting order out of chaos and putting the animals back in the cars or cages. Where the vehicles were damaged the animals were doubled up.

A lion cage on a wrecked flat car was being eased off by means of ropes and pulley, the tawny beast inside giving vent to his displeasure in growls and roars.

"Some class to this film; eh?" cried Joe.

"That's right," agreed his chum. "I'm sorry for the trouble, and for the hurt animals, and I'm glad none of the folks was killed, but it sure is a dandy chance for us."

"Look!" suddenly cried Joe. "That lion cage has gotten away from 'em!"

As he spoke, Blake saw the cage beginning to run rapidly down the planks that had been laid to get it from the car to the ground. A rope had broken.

"Hold it!" cried the circus man.

But it was too late. With a rumble and crash the cage slid down to the ground, struck some obstruction, and the next moment toppled over on its side. There was a splintering of wood, a door flew open, and the big lion bounded out with a roar of defiance.

"Wow!" cried Joe. "Look at that!"

"A great chance!" exclaimed Blake, coolly. "We'll film him!" and he proceeded to grind away at the crank as if he were making views of a most peaceful scene.

There came a scream from the direction of the theatrical car, and Joe, looking, saw a number of ladies scrambling for the doors. The sight of the freed lion had been too much for them.

There was a scattering of the circus men, too, at the sight of the tawny beast standing near the broken cage and lashing its sides with its tufted tail.

"Get after him, boys!" cried the circus manager.

"Not for mine!" replied several.

"Cowards vot you are!" cried a new voice, and through the widening circle of wagon handlers stalked a man—evidently a German animal trainer. He carried a long whip, which he cracked viciously. At the snap the lion winced.

"Down, King!" cried the man. "Down!"

Once more the lion cringed, and then began to whimper.

"You see how gentle he is—cowards vot you are!" sneered the man.

He approached the great beast fearlessly, the lion, with shifting eyes, meanwhile following the man.

"I lead him," went on the German. "There iss no harm in King; is dere, olt fellow?" and he actually patted the head of the great beast.

"Good, Herr Kilngert!" cried the manager. "Now you men bring up an empty cage," and when it was rolled near the lion, the trainer actually led the beast in by its mane.

"See, cowards vot you are!" he sneered at the men, as he shut the door after him, leaving the lion to raise its voice in a mournful groan at losing the short liberty it had enjoyed.

"This is great!" cried Joe.

"The best ever," asserted his chum.

The work of caring for the liberated animals went on rapidly. Only a few were loose now, and none of them dangerous. Still the scene was a lively one, for the railroad men were busy, and the boys made nearly a thousand-foot reel of it all, the camera, fortunately, having been fully loaded.

Just then the circus manager noticed them, and started in some surprise.

"What are you fellows doing?" he asked, striding toward them.

"Filming this wreck," replied Blake, calmly.

"Making moving pictures; eh?"

"That's it," said Joe, looking to see how much film remained to expose.

"Did you get that lion scene?"

"We did."

"Did; eh? Well, you've got pluck, all right. I wouldn't want everybody to know it, but that's one of the most dangerous lions in captivity. He's killed several of his keepers, and only this German seems able to manage him. No wonder the men held back. And so you filmed him; eh?"

"Oh, we're used to thrills," said Blake, with a smile, as the last of the film was reeled off.

"So I should judge," observed the circus man. "Say," he went on, "I've been looking for some young fellows with nerve, and I guess I've found 'em. How would you like to go into the circus business?"

"I'm afraid we can't consider it," spoke Joe. "We have something else on hand. We leave for Africa in about a week."

"What for; to get pictures?"

"No, to get my sister, who is a missionary helper there."

"To Africa!" exclaimed the circus man. "Say, this is just the opportunity I've been looking for! Boys, I've got a great proposition to lay before you. I'll see you in a little while—just as soon as I can straighten things out. Hi there!" he called, suddenly. "Don't let that elephant hurt that camel. Separate 'em, men! Lively there!" and he rushed over to where the two animals seemed on the point of coming to a clash.

CHAPTER V
OFF FOR AFRICA

"WHAT SORT OF AN offer do you think he's going to make us, Blake?" asked Joe, as they finished the films of the circus wreck, and began taking their camera apart.

"I haven't the least idea, unless he wants to buy a reel of these pictures to show in his circus; and yet I don't see how he can do that very well."

"Oh, if he wants to buy a reel, I suppose we can sell it to him, after we run off some positives."

"Sure, we're in that business. But let's get back and see what the chances are for moving. The wreck isn't as bad as I feared it was."

"No, and a good thing, too."

"I sure thought it was all up with us, when that crash came," went on Blake. "It sounded like the end of everything."

"That's right. And when Miss Lee yelled 'Snake!' I didn't know what to make of it."

"Thought it was a sort of nightmare; eh?"

"That's about it."

The boys found the excitement much lessened when they got back to their car. It was occupied by a number of other passengers from the rest of the train, most of them women, but with a few men, who seemed a bit uneasy. The women made no effort to disguise their nervousness.

"Are all—ahem! are all the wild—that is to say—is there any more danger, young men?" asked a portly gentleman, as Blake and Joe entered the car.

"No, the only animals loose now are a camel and an elephant, and the men will soon have them back in the train," replied Joe.

"Ah! I am glad to hear that," replied the man. "I—er—was just going out to offer my services. I used to be somewhat of a hunter, but—er—if they are all captured there is no need of my going—"

"Don't you dare go, Henry!" cried a little woman, clinging to his coat tails. "I don't want you all chewed up by a lion. Don't you dare to leave me."

"I—I won't, Martha," he answered. "I'll stay and protect you."

"Humph!" exclaimed C. C. "I guess there was not much danger of Henry going—not yet."

Several of the men from the other cars looked relieved at the news the boys brought in, and soon, having ascertained by observation that no animals, save a few horses, were loose, they left, taking their women folk with them.

"I guess they used this car as a sort of haven of refuge, while the animals were loose," observed Mr. Hadley, while Blake and Joe put away their camera.

"That's right," remarked Mr. Duncan, who had gone outside to see Joe and his chum operate the machine. "That's why the railroad men wanted those people to come in here. It's a steel car and safe from attack."

"There wasn't any danger," declared Blake. "The lion was the only dangerous one, and his trainer made him as meek as a lamb. It was a wonderful exhibition."

"That's right," agreed Joe. "Once more our hoodoo—of something always happening—seems to have us in charge. I hope it will keep right on until we get to Africa and find Jessie. That would be the best luck ever."

"Indeed, it would," agreed his father.

The work of clearing away the wreck went on rapidly. Fortunately, the smash had taken place near a small way station, and men from it, as well as inhabitants of a nearby town, came out to lend their aid.

As it happened, only the rear end of the circus train had been hit, a few cars being smashed. Of course, the jar and crash, however, had been communicated all along the length of it. The passenger engine was considerably damaged, as was the baggage car and the coach directly behind it, but the locomotive could still be used, though not for great speed.

An examination of the baggage of the theatrical troupe showed it had suffered only a little, none of the moving picture cameras having been damaged.

Nor were many persons hurt. None was in serious condition, and their injuries were dressed by a physician who chanced to be on the train. The first-aid kit carried by the theatrical company proved very useful.

As for the circus people, none of them was hurt, though some were badly shaken up and bruised. A few animals were killed, but none of the valuable ones, and soon all that had escaped or strayed were safe in other cages or cars.

"All aboard!" called the passenger conductor, after straightening out many tangles and wiring on ahead for another train to meet his. The theatrical car could be used, but it was considered safer to get another as soon as possible. "All aboard!"

"If that circus man wants to tell us about some big proposition he has, he'd better hurry," remarked Joe, looking out of the window to where he could see

Mr. Stone directing the work of securing the cages on the flat cars. "We'll be moving soon."

"That's right," agreed Blake. "I wonder what he can want us to do? I'm not going to be a circus performer, I give you that straight."

"Me either," declared Joe.

Evidently Mr. Stone attached some importance to the message he had for the moving picture boys, for no sooner did he hear the orders given to get ready to move the passenger train than, leaving the finishing of the circus work to an assistant, he hurried to the theatrical car.

"Well, boys," he began, "I suppose you have been wondering what it was I wanted to see you about?"

"Somewhat," admitted Joe.

"I'll come to the point at once," went on Mr. Stone. "I liked the nerve you boys showed when that lion got out, and, as I said, I've been wanting for some time to get in touch with such lads. It takes nerve, this circus business."

"But we don't want to get into the circus business," interposed Blake. "As my chum here told you, we are going to the jungles of Africa to find his sister."

"That's all right," said Mr. Stone. "What I have to propose will fit right in with that. You know how to take moving pictures; don't you?"

"If they don't, no one in the business does!" exclaimed Mr. Hadley. "They're experts at it. They can get anything."

"Good! I'm glad to hear it. Do you think they could get views of the animals in the jungle—views that would show the animals in their native wilds—fighting, feeding at the water holes—just as they actually are, undisturbed by man? Could they do that?"

"Of course they could!" exclaimed the head photographer, while Joe and Blake looked curiously at each other.

"Then they're just the very lads I want!" exclaimed Mr. Stone. "Listen. For some time back I have been considering the showing of films of wild animals of the jungle in connection with my circus. I have a big menagerie, as you have doubtless noticed. People are always interested in animals.

"Now, if I could fit up a dark tent with my show and exhibit films of wild animals as they are in the jungle, people could look at them, and then, by stepping into the next tent, they could see the very animals themselves—at least, some just like those in the pictures. I think it would make a hit."

"It does sound good," remarked Mr. Ringold, with a theatrical man's insight into what would please the public.

"It's going to be good!" declared Mr. Stone. "Now, if you boys will make the films, I'll do the rest. What do you say; is it a go? I'll pay you what's right, and the only stipulation is that I am to have an interest in the films, for we can doubtless sell a number of the reels. Will you do it?"

Joe and Blake hesitated. The idea appealed to them. Joe looked at his father.

"I don't see why you can't do this," said Mr. Duncan. "We have to go to the jungle, anyhow, to find Jessie, and there's nothing to hinder you from taking moving pictures. I think you may accept the offer."

"That's the way to talk!" exclaimed Mr. Stone.

"Shall we, Blake?" asked Joe.

"I'm willing."

"Then it's a go!" cried his chum. "We'll do the best we can for you, Mr. Stone."

"Good!" cried the circus man. "Now you're going to New York, as I understand it. You'll probably be there a week, won't you, before you can complete your arrangements for going to Africa?"

"Probably," replied Mr. Duncan.

"All right. I'll come on before then and look you up. I've got to go on with the circus for a time, and then my helpers can look after it. I want to be in New York, anyhow, to see about suing the railroad, and that will just fit in. That's all settled, then? You'll get pictures for me of the wild animals of the jungle?"

"We'll do our best," promised Joe and Blake.

"Then I'll see you later and arrange details. Good-bye."

"All aboard!" called the passenger conductor again, and the train, somewhat crippled, pulled away from the scene of the wreck.

"Well, what do you know about that?" asked Joe of his chum, when they had settled down, nursing some minor cuts and bruises. "Isn't that about the limit—filming wild animals in the jungle!"

"It sounds strange, but it's reasonable, I suppose."

"If you got films of the fanatical Indians, I don't see why you can't get wild animals," said Mr. Duncan. "It can't be much harder than getting the wreck in which I came ashore."

"But it's more dangerous," said C. C. Piper, in his most melancholy voice. "Think of standing beside a camera, grinding away at the handle, with a rogue elephant charging at you; or a big rhinoceros. Not for mine! You'll never come back alive!"

"Oh, don't say such horrid things!" cried Miss Lee. "You are worse than ever, Gloomy."

"Well, it's so. They'll have a terrible time. I wouldn't go for a fortune. New York for mine. We'll probably be dead when we get there, but we'll get there."

"Oh, go get something to eat," advised Mr. Ringold. "That may put you in better humor."

"I guess I will," agreed C. C. "But I'll probably get indigestion from the fright I've had."

New York was reached without incident, and the boys went to their boarding house, Mr. Duncan accompanying them. The theatrical troupe separated, all promising to see our heroes before the trip to Africa was started. Macaroni, or Charles Anderson, the thin young helper of Joe and Blake, did not come from the coast with them, having obtained a position in a San Francisco moving picture theatre.

Busy days followed, considerable preparation being necessary to prepare for the African trip. In due time Mr. Stone arrived in New York, and made satisfactory arrangements with Joe and Blake for taking pictures of wild animals.

"Mind," he explained, "I want pictures so that the person seeing them will imagine he's right on the spot looking at the animals eating, fighting, or playing about. Don't let the animals pose for you."

"I guess there's not much danger," said Blake, with a laugh. "A wild lion posing would be a curious sight."

"And one not altogether healthy for the moving picture machine and the fellow operating it," added Blake.

"Well, it's all settled, then," concluded Mr. Stone, and a contract was drawn up.

Good-byes were said to the theatrical company—that is, all but Mr. Piper, who, so Mr. Ringold said, had gone off on a little trip. The boys left their farewells for him.

Then, the arrangements being completed, they went aboard their vessel in New York, and soon were on their way to Africa, Naples being the first stopping point.

"Ho! for the jungle!" cried Blake, as he stood on deck while the ship went through the Narrows.

"And for my little sister!" added Joe, softly.

CHAPTER VI
AN OLD FRIEND

BLAKE AND JOE SOON made friends aboard the ship. They were lively lads, and as soon as it became known they were on voyage to Africa they were asked many questions.

They did not give details of their two quests, merely saying that they were on their way to see Joe's sister, and, incidentally, to get views of the jungle animals.

"There's no use telling them we haven't seen my sister in so many years," suggested Joe, who was a bit sensitive on the subject. "And if we go into too many details about those wild animals they'll think we're faking."

"That's right," agreed Blake.

The fact that they had with them moving picture cameras, and film, and were experts in their use, soon became known all through the ship, and they received many requests to take views of the passengers at various deck games.

This they did, but as there were no facilities aboard for developing and printing the films, the pictures could not be shown. However, the boys left the negatives with the captain, who promised to have them ready for any passengers who made a return trip with him.

For themselves, however, Joe and Blake got some fine views of a storm at sea, the waves being exceptionally high. The vessel rolled and rocked so that it was hard for the lads to keep their footing, but they were not seasick, which was more than could be said of most of the passengers.

"In fact, there's one gentleman who hasn't been out of his stateroom since we started," said the commander. "He wanted me to stop the ship, or else turn back, when we struck the first bit of open water. But you boys are real sailors."

Mr. Duncan, of course, was at home on the water, and he spent much of his time in company with the officers of the craft, swapping "yarns" of the deep.

Joe and Blake spent some days looking over their moving picture cameras. They had purchased a new one in place of one of their old ones—a machine with several improvements.

As I have designed this book to be instructive as well as entertaining, I will give a brief description of how the moving picture machine works.

I presume you all know what a camera is. It consists of a light-tight box, with a lens for properly focusing whatever is to be taken. Back of the lens is a sensitized film of celluloid or a glass plate. When the image has been taken on this film, it is developed by chemicals, and when dry a print or "positive" can be made from it. And, for all this simplicity, it is a very wonderful process.

A moving picture camera is merely another snapshot camera on a larger scale, except that instead of one plate back of the lens there is a continuous band, or celluloid roll. By turning a handle the reel of film passes behind the lens at the rate of sixteen small plates per second, taking this number of views of whatever moving or animated scene it is desired to show. A shutter, worked by the handle, alternately opens and closes just as you work the shutter of your small camera by pressing a button, and this shutter cuts off the view while a new section of film is pulled into place behind the lens.

A moving picture camera can take pictures on a thousand feet of celluloid reel at one operation, and as each picture is only three-quarters of an inch wide, you can see that quite a number of separate views are possible.

So much for taking the moving pictures. The operator points his camera at whatever he wants to show—a speeding train, a man diving, a scene in a theatre—anything he wants—turns the handle, and the rest is automatic.

When the reel is filled with pictures it is developed just as you would develop a single plate, or film, except, of course, a larger tank is necessary.

Many persons suppose that the film that is in the moving picture camera is the same one that is run through the projecting machine, and thrown on the screen. That is not so, otherwise it would be necessary to take many hundreds of reels of the same scene, to accommodate the many theatres.

The first film taken is called a "negative" and is a sort of "master film." Once this is dry it is put in an apparatus somewhat like the camera. Under the master film, just as you put a piece of sensitive paper under your one negative, is a reel of unexposed film. A bright light is placed in front, the machinery starts pulling the strip of celluloid along, and from the negative any number of "positives" can be made. It is these positives, with the true relation of lights and shadows, that are thrown on the screen.

The positive is put on the projecting machine, an intense electric light is used, again a handle is turned, and the views, magnified many hundred times, are thrown on the screen.

For the explanation of why "moving pictures move," or seem to, though they really do not, I refer readers to the first book of this series, where a full explanation is given, with a short history of how moving pictures were discovered.

But I know you boys and girls want to get on with this story, so I will save further explanations for another time.

After Blake and Joe had made their pictures of the storm they got quite a surprise. They had put away their camera, and were talking with Mr. Duncan in their stateroom, when a steward knocked at the door.

"Well?" asked Blake.

"If you please, sir," the man announced, "there is a friend of yours who wants to see you."

"A friend of ours?" asked Joe.

"Yes, sir. On board here. He says he's an old friend?"

"An old friend? We haven't any old friends on board here," said Blake, wondering if his rival, Munson, who was later his friend, could be on the ship.

"Yes, he says so, and he wants you to come and see him before he dies."

"Before he dies!" cried Joe.

"Well, he thinks he is dying—all seasick folks do," replied the steward. "I will take you to him," and the boys, much surprised, followed to a nearby stateroom.

As they opened the door they heard a familiar voice saying:

"Oh, why did I do it? Oh, why did I ever come? Oh, this is the last of me! Let me see my friends before I go. Oh, dear!"

"Listen!" cried Blake.

"If it isn't C. C. Piper I'm an Indian!" exclaimed Joe.

"Yes, look your last on me, boys," said the gloomy comedian, as he raised his head from the berth. "I'm a goner!"

CHAPTER VII
BAD NEWS

BLAKE AND JOE HARDLY knew whether to believe the evidence of their senses or not. To all appearances there, before them, in a narrow bunk, was C. C. Piper, the erstwhile comedian of the theatrical troupe. And yet, as they looked at him again, they saw a great change in him. He was wan, thin, and pale—altogether ill-looking.

"Is—is it really him?" gasped Joe. "It doesn't seem—"

"I hardly know," began Blake, "and yet—"

"It's me, all right, boys," answered Mr. Piper, and they recognized his voice, weak as it was.

"His name is Piper," put in the steward, "and he's down that way on the passenger list."

"But I won't be here long," groaned C. C. "I haven't much longer to live, boys. That's why I sent for you."

"They all imagine that," whispered the steward to Joe and Blake. "It's only a bad case of sea-sickness. He'll be over it soon. The doctor has given him some stuff. But they all imagine they're going to die, and some of 'em are afraid they won't. He will be up eating as hearty as an elephant soon."

"Never!" cried C. C., gloomily. "I'll never eat again," but, even as he spoke he seemed to have gained a little in hope, since the boys had come to see him. Blake decided to solve the mystery.

"How under the sun did you come here?" he asked. "The last we heard of you was that you had taken a few days' vacation."

"I decided to take a longer one," said Mr. Piper, his voice growing stronger. "When I got away from the theatrical crowd I just couldn't bear to go back. I had some money saved up, and the idea of doing more moving picture dramas was distasteful to me. So I just decided to go to Africa with you boys."

"Go to Africa with us!" cried Joe.

"Yes. You won't object; will you? I'll pay my own way, and I may be able to help you. I used to be a good shot, and I have traveled considerable. I've been in India, and shot lions and tigers, to say nothing of elephants."

"You have!" exclaimed Blake, with a new admiration for the actor.

"Yes, I know something of big game, though not in Africa. Let me go along."

"I haven't any objections," spoke Blake, rather glad, on the whole, that C. C. was along. In spite of his gloom he could be jolly at times.

"Me either," added Joe. "But how did you happen to come here, and we not know it?"

"Well, I decided to make it a sort of surprise," said the actor. "I learned which ship you were sailing on, and engaged passage. I asked the purser and captain to keep my name off the list until the last minute, and they did; so you never saw it. I intended to keep to my room, or at best go out on deck only at night, until we got to the other side. I was afraid your father might object," he said to Joe.

"I guess he'll be glad to have some one along who knows how to shoot," spoke the boy. "Blake and I aren't much with guns."

"Well," went on C. C., "the storm was too much for me. I was afraid I might die, and I wanted to see you before I went. So I sent for you; but, I declare, I feel better already."

"That's always the way!" declared the steward. "You had better have something to eat."

"Eat! Ugh—er—I think I will!" cried Mr. Piper. "It may kill me, but I might as well die that way as starve. Bring me a good meal, steward," and as the man left C. C. told the boys how he had secretly purchased his ticket, and had sent a note to Mr. Ringold, telling the theatrical man that he would have to get another comedian.

"It won't make much difference to him," said Mr. Piper. "Business is going to be dull for a time, and he can easily get some one in my place if he likes. When we come back, after we get your sister," he said to Joe, "I can take my old place. But I don't want to see a moving picture for a year."

"We expect to take some," said Blake, with a smile.

"But not dramas!" cried C. C.

"No, just wild animals, and perhaps scenes with the African natives," spoke Joe.

"That's all right," said Mr. Piper, and his meal having arrived, he sat up to it with a relish. The boys could see that he would be all right soon, and left to tell Mr. Duncan the surprising news.

"Why, no, I haven't any objection to his accompanying us," said Joe's father, when it had been related to him. "In fact, I think he will be an advantage. I was thinking of hiring some sort of a hunter to accompany us, for if we have to go into the jungle we'll need the services of a good shot. As it is, I think we will have to hire a guide—a white man—who will know how to handle the native porters. It will be necessary to take someone like that with us."

"I wish the time would pass!" exclaimed Joe. "I'm anxious to get into the jungle and film an elephant charging, or a lion rushing at us."

"Yes, as long as he doesn't rush too close," put in Blake. "I'm thinking it's going to be ticklish work standing up to a charging lion."

The next day Mr. Piper was well enough to leave his room. He called on Mr. Duncan, apologized for the unconventional manner in which he had attached himself to the party, and was made welcome.

Then, for several days, nothing was talked of but the coming trip into the jungle. Mr. Piper's experiences in India would serve them all in good stead, it was felt.

"The three worst animals in Africa," he said, "are the elephant, lion and rhinoceros. Some put the cape buffalo in place of the elephant, and I don't know but what they are right, in certain sections."

"How is that?" asked Blake.

"Because you never can tell what they are going to do," was the answer. "From what I have read I should put the rhinoceros down as the most dangerous."

"Why?" Joe wanted to know.

"Because he seems to act wholly without reason. You never can tell when one is going to rush on you, and the charge of one of the ungainly beasts is no joke. You see, their eyesight, like that of the elephant, is very poor. They depend altogether on their hearing and sense of smell, both of which are very acute. Once they scent, or hear, what they think is an enemy they charge blindly. Their rush, their great weight and the ripping power of their horns is enormous. Natives have been impaled through their hip bones by rhinoceroses, and tossed into the jungle to die, merely because they passed by a place where a rhino was sleeping.

"So you never can tell what they may do. You may pass one without the least intention of harming it, but it may blindly rush you, and, if you don't stop it with a bullet, you are likely to be killed.

"Buffaloes are much the same, but they are less erratic. You can more easily figure on what they will do. Elephants and lions will seldom charge, unless you persistently hunt them. They prefer to run along and mind their own affairs. Rhinos and buffaloes do not. But we'll see what happens when we get to the jungle, boys."

"Oh, I do hope we can get some good pictures!" exclaimed Blake, and Joe echoed the desire.

The voyage passed off without incident. They made a stop of a few days in Naples, and inspected some of the Italian moving picture studios. Of late, several Italian firms had entered the business, making elaborate films of historical subjects, and Joe and Blake were interested in noting their methods.

"But they all have to come to the United States for one thing," said Blake, after a tour of one of the largest factories.

"What's that?" asked Joe.

"The perforations in the edges of the film, by which it is moved in the camera or projector. They all have to conform to the standard adopted by Thomas A. Edison, when he first turned out a moving picture."

This is a well-known fact; all films, whether domestic or foreign, have the same number of perforations per inch, on each side of the film, as that adopted by the celebrated inventor of West Orange, New Jersey, several years ago. It is a tribute to an American genius, and the boys, though so far from home, felt a sense of nearness as they wandered through the Italian studio and saw the Edison standard perforation gauge being used.

From Naples they took another German line steamer for Suez, thence to go to Mombasa. Now they began to get sight of foreigners other than Europeans, for there were both African and East Indians aboard, and there were many interesting sights.

Nothing of importance occurred until reaching Suez, and there more foreign types were noticed. And it was here that they received their first bad news.

They were just about to embark for the last stage of their journey, to Mombasa, when Joe and Blake came aboard with a copy of an English paper printed there. They were idly scanning the news, hoping to see something from their own land, when Joe uttered a cry, as he stared at a certain paragraph.

"What is it?" asked Blake.

"Bad news," replied his chum. "I wonder if we can keep this from Dad?"

He pointed to few lines, which read:

"Latest advices from Entebbe state that the native uprisings at Kargos, a missionary station, are more serious than at first supposed. The whole missionary settlement was wiped out, and the missionaries, a Mr. Brown and his wife, were taken into the interior by the natives. It is understood that the Home Office will take immediate action, though the missionaries were United States subjects. The American consul has made an appeal for help."

"That's fierce!" cried Joe. "That's where my sister was—at Kargos, near Entebbe. Now she's been carried off into the jungle."

"It doesn't say so," spoke Blake, clinging to a last hope.

"No, but if Mr. and Mrs. Brown have been carried off, it is likely that Jessie went with them. This sure is tough!"

"What is?" asked Mr. Duncan, as he approached the lads. Joe tried to hide the paper, but too late.

CHAPTER VIII
INTO THE INTERIOR

FOR A MOMENT JOE and Blake did not know whether or not to tell Mr. Duncan what they had seen in the paper. Then the realization came to Joe that he could not hope to conceal from his father the bad news.

"We're up against it, Dad!" he exclaimed, with a brave attempt to pass it off.

"How's that, son?"

"Jessie is gone!"

"Gone?" There was alarm in Mr. Duncan's tone.

"Yes, the mission station where she was with Mr. and Mrs. Brown has been raided by the natives, and they have been carried into the jungle."

Mr. Duncan looked stunned for a moment, and then exclaimed:

"Into the jungle! My poor little girl! But we'll go into the interior after her. Joe, we'll get her away from the savages, if it's at all possible!"

"That's what we will!" cried the brother of the missing girl.

"And I'm with you!" added Blake.

"Count me in on that!" said another voice, and they turned to behold C. C. Piper.

"I heard what you said," went on the actor. "Don't be discouraged. We'll get her, all right. Those natives may not be half so bad as they're painted, and they may treat your sister and the missionaries fairly decent.

"What if they are in the jungle? We can follow them. I didn't learn to shoot big game for nothing. We'll trek into the interior; the sooner the better. It will all come out right yet, you'll see!"

This talk, so much in contrast with the way C. C. usually spoke, had its effect. Joe, Blake and Mr. Duncan felt more hopeful.

"It's like the time on the beach," whispered Blake. "It seems that when there's an emergency C. C. jumps into it and forgets his gloom."

"That's right," agreed Joe. "It may come back to him, but, for the time being, he's jollier than usual, and I'm glad of it."

"So am I," said Mr. Duncan, for he knew something of C. C. Piper.

"If only we could make faster time!" exclaimed Mr. Duncan, when they were once more under way. "It seems that I never knew a steamer to make such slow progress."

"And yet we are doing fairly well," said C. C. "Now, have you formed any plans?"

"I don't seem to be able to," went on Jessie's father, as he once more scanned the paper giving an account of the raid on the missionary station. "Only the fact that my little girl may be among the savages appeals to me. Oh, if we could only rescue her!"

"We will!" declared Blake, with a confidence he did not altogether feel. "We'll get right among 'em, and if we have to scare 'em with a moving picture machine, telling 'em it's the worst kind of witch-medicine, we'll do it."

"If only we can influence 'em in some way!" murmured Joe.

"Now as to plans," went on Mr. Piper, who seemed ready to take practical charge of the expedition, which was likely to have a harder task before it than at first supposed. "I think that our best work can be done by going direct to Mombasa, as we figured on originally. There we can take the Uganda railroad to the Victoria Nyanza. Crossing that body of water we can get to Entebbe, and from there—"

"From there we'll have to strike into the jungle, try to locate the station at Kargos and, and then—" began Mr. Duncan.

"And then find Jessie!" interrupted Joe.

"And we'll do it!" cried Blake.

"My idea exactly!" declared C. C. Piper, who seemed to show no disposition to revert to his original state of gloom.

"I wonder if we'll get any chance to make moving pictures for that circus man?" mused Joe. "Not that I'm even going to think about it until we find Jessie, but—".

"You'll probably have plenty of chance," said Mr. Piper. "The railroad journey is five hundred and eighty miles, and we can't make it all in one day. There will be frequent stops, I expect, and on them you can make moving pictures."

"But will there be wild animals near the railroad?" asked Blake.

"There certainly will," declared the actor. "It runs right to Port Florence, on Victoria Lake, and I have often read of the trainmen seeing anything from elephants to lions along the track, for it runs through a big game preserve. Why, there is one story of a German hunter who went down on a special car on the Uganda railroad to kill a man-eating lion that had been terrorizing the natives near one of the line stations. An Englishman and an Italian were with him. The car was shunted to a siding on the railroad near where the lion had been seen.

"It was hot, the Englishman sat by an open window to watch for the lion, but fell asleep. The Italian stretched out on the floor, and the German got into a bunk. The Italian was roused by a commotion, and awoke to see the lion standing on him with his hind feet, while his fore paws were on the seat where the Englishman had been. The latter was dead.

"The German jumped out of his bunk directly on the lion, that leaped out of the car through a window, taking the body of the Englishman with him. I don't know whether they got that lion or not, but if you think there aren't any wild animals near the railroad you have another guess."

"Whew!" whistled Blake. "If it's like that we may get pictures yet."

"I guess so," said Joe, but even this thought could not make him forget his sister.

The trip to Mombasa was without incident, and they were soon dropping anchor in that beautiful harbor. It is an ancient African city, and the boys and their companions found many Englishmen there as well as some of their own countrymen. They put up at a hotel, and on making inquiries learned where best to apply to be fitted out for a trip into the interior. They had, besides their personal baggage, their moving picture cameras, and a considerable quantity of film.

"And now, since we know we may have a brush with the natives," said Joe, "we'll have to get arms."

"Yes, indeed," agreed C. C. "And I want a heavy hunting rifle. I'm out after big game, though it may get me—. Oh, I don't mean that!" he cried hastily. "I'm going to try not to be gloomy on this trip," and he smiled reassuringly.

Our friends were fortunate enough to obtain the services of a veteran hunter and guide, a Sergeant Hotchkiss, who had fought in the Boer war. He agreed to accompany them into the interior, and to arrange for a safari once they reached Lake Nyanza.

"But you had better bargain for your provisions and supplies here," he said; "that is, all but the meat, which you will have to shoot as you want it. You're going to a good game country."

This was done, and, about a week after arriving at Mombasa, Joe, Blake and the little party took a train on the Uganda railroad, their supplies, cameras, films and other things going with them.

"Off for the jungle!" cried Blake, as they pulled out of the station. "Into the interior."

"For Jessie and the wild animal pictures," added Joe. "But it's Jessie first!"

"That's right!" cried his father.

CHAPTER IX
THE SAFARI

THE QUEER ENGLISH-STYLE COACHES, specially made to afford protection against the tropical sun; the odd little engine and many other things about the railroad through Africa, making it much different from the lines in the United States, caused the moving picture boys, Mr. Duncan and C. C. Piper no small amount of wonder at first. Everything seemed to be done contrary to what it was in their country.

"But you'll generally find," said Sergeant Hotchkiss, with pardonable pride in his nation's progress, "that we get along fairly well over here."

"That's right," agreed Blake. And when they came to think of a railroad actually being built through part of the former "Dark Continent," where, until comparatively recently, no white man had ever set foot, they marveled.

"The British government," went on the sergeant, "has made this a game preserve, almost up to the line of the railroad, in fact, with the idea of having travelers, who wish to, see nature at its wildest and as it really is. Nearly all game is protected, and licenses have to be procured to shoot a certain number of each species."

"We don't need any," said Joe, "for all we're going to do is to shoot 'em with our moving picture machines."

"Unless they attack us," said C. C., as he examined one of the several rifles he had purchased for himself and the boys. "That's allowed; isn't it, sergeant?"

"Oh, yes, to protect life. You may shoot anything, then."

"A lion for mine!" cried Blake.

"I'd rather get an elephant and save the tusks," spoke Joe, while C. C. said:

"Well, I'd like to bag a big rhino with horns about a yard long. The head would make a stunning ornament for my den, but I suppose if I went after one I'd be bagged by it and the horn would be stuck through me, so—"

"Hold on!" cried Mr. Duncan, with a smile. "I thought you had given up that sort of talk."

"So I have!" declared C. C. "No more gloom for me; if I forget, remind me of it."

"Let's talk about filming the wild animals," suggested Joe.

"Oh, you won't have any lack of subjects," declared Sergeant Hotchkiss. "Sometimes certain game becomes so numerous and so bold that it is taken off the protected list and classed as vermin, when anyone is allowed to shoot at will. Often here the buffaloes and hippos are so styled, for the latter often come in from the lakes and rivers and destroy the natives' crops. And it has happened that the buffaloes get so bold that they attack on the least, and often without any, provocation."

It did not take long for the train to reach a wild part of the country, passing through what would be a jungle, except that it was reclaimed to civilization by the railroad line. On either side of the rails, a short distance away, it was a real jungle, teeming with bird and animal life.

It was on the afternoon of the second day, and the boys had gotten their moving picture cameras in readiness. They had begun to despair of seeing any big game, in spite of what the sergeant had said, until they got farther into the jungle, for the most they had glimpsed were big birds and a hyena or two, the latter slinking off at the approach of the train before they could be filmed.

Suddenly the engine began to slacken speed, and finally came to a stop, nowhere near a station.

"What's that?" asked Blake, as he finished threading a film into his camera.

"Maybe a rhino on the track," suggested the sergeant. "We did hit one once, and damaged the engine so we couldn't go on. But I don't think that's the case now. However, we'll take a look."

They piled out of the coach. It was hot, and moisture hung in the air. There was a deadly overpowering odor—a jungle smell. Great ferns made a thick foliage, and back amid the trees the queer notes of strange birds could be heard, while, now and then, a movement in the grass indicated the passage of some larger creature of the hidden fastness.

"Something's up!" exclaimed Joe, as he saw the conductor, fireman and engineer of the train in consultation.

"Telegraph line is down," said Sergeant Hotchkiss. "I can see where a pole has fallen. We can't go on until it's mended—can't get the proper orders, you see."

"What made it come down?" asked Joe.

"Don't know—we'll find out," was the answer.

"Probably the pole was set in a swamp," observed C. C., as they walked forward.

"Not at all!" exclaimed the conductor, who had made friends with the boys. "It's an odd case, and if you lads had been here with your cameras you'd have had a fine chance for a picture. Nothing less than a giraffe knocked our telegraph fine out of business!"

"A giraffe!" cried Blake, wondering whether the conductor was "stringing" him.

"That's it. You can see his hoof marks where he passed over the railroad. His head was so high that his neck probably hit the wire, and, as neither the wire nor the neck would break the pole had to. Yes, take my word for it, a giraffe broke down the line, and we'll be held up until it can be fixed."

"How long will that be?" asked Blake, an idea coming into his head.

"Oh, several hours, maybe. I'll have to send a man back on foot to the next station to have a lineman come out. I don't dare take the chance of proceeding without orders, for there is no telling when a special might come along and run into us."

"Then, if we've got several hours," cried Blake, "can't we go off into the jungle and try for some pictures?"

"Great!" exclaimed Joe.

"I think you might," said the conductor. "Don't go too far, though. I'll have the engineer whistle about an hour before we are to start, and you can then come back."

The boys agreed to do this, and with Sergeant Hotchkiss to act as guide, and with C. C. to serve in the capacity of guard with his gun, Joe and Blake set out with their cameras, Mr. Duncan deciding to stay in the train.

"I do hope we stir up a lion!" exclaimed Blake, as they trudged along a trail made by the natives. Whither it led they did not know, but they had not gone far before Mr. Hotchkiss called a halt, and, pointing to a wide path leading across the narrow trail—a path seemingly forced by some large body—said:

"Buffaloes!"

"Are they around here?" asked Joe, thinking of what he had heard of these savage creatures with their immense horns.

"It's hard to say," replied the sergeant. "Best to be careful."

They decided to follow the buffalo path, which was one literally smashed through the dense jungle growth, as they hoped to come to some open space where the creatures might be feeding, and so get a picture.

Luck was with them, for they had not gone more than a mile before the sergeant, who was in the lead, exclaimed:

"Here you are, boys!"

Joe and Blake pressed forward, and, coming suddenly into a sort of glade where the grass grew tall, they saw a score or more of the big cape buffaloes. Some were lying down, others standing up, and some feeding, while one big bull seemed to be on guard. The wind was blowing from the creatures to the boys—the man-odor would not carry to the animals.

"If we can get a little nearer we can film them," whispered Joe.

"Go ahead," counseled Blake, and they stole forward with one camera.

"Plucky lads," observed the sergeant, admiringly.

"That's what," admitted C. C., as he looked to his gun. Perhaps he wished for a chance to use it.

Getting a good position the moving picture camera was set up, and soon, with Joe to steady it, Blake began turning the handle. With the first click all the buffaloes who were lying down got up and faced toward the boys. They saw them, but the wind being contrary did not give them the smell they needed, and they watched warily and curiously.

"Look out! If they start for you—run," advised the sergeant.

The whole herd of buffaloes now began moving about restlessly, and this was just what the boys wanted, for moving pictures that do not move are not much of a success. Then the big bull, with a switch of his tail and an angry snort, started toward the lads.

"Look out!" cried the sergeant. "Run!"

Hardly had he spoken than the whole herd was in motion, but the lads, far from running, stood their ground.

"This is just what we want!" cried Joe. "It will make a dandy film!"

"Yes, we can take views for a few seconds more," decided Blake. They did not know the dangerous quality of the buffalo, or they would not have risked this.

"Run! Run!" cried the sergeant. "Oh, why didn't I bring a gun. They'll be killed!"

"No they won't!" declared C. C., as he knelt down to take aim at the foremost bull with a heavy elephant gun.

"Come on!" fairly screamed the sergeant, for he knew the terrible power of the buffalo's horns.

"I guess we've got enough," cried Blake. "Grab the tripod, Joe, and I'll take the camera!"

The tripod, made for quick detachment, was slipped off by Joe, and together the two lads made back-tracks. The buffaloes were coming on.

"Crack!" snapped out C. C.'s gun, and it was seen that he had not boasted vainly of his prowess. The big bull seemed to crumple up, and turned a complete somersault.

Whether it was this queer action on his part, or whether the herd did not like the sound of the gun, was not made manifest. At any rate, they stopped, and, after waiting a moment, they wheeled around and retreated—that is, all but the big bull. He had been killed.

"A dandy shot!" exclaimed the sergeant, admiringly.

"I wish I had time to get his head," said C. C., regretfully. As the other buffaloes disappeared, the boys walked up to look at the creature. Truly he was a large and fine specimen, and they took some pictures of it to finish out their film.

They went on for some distance farther, but saw nothing worth taking. Then the engine whistle blew, and they started back. On the return they passed a water hole, and from a screen of bushes some views were taken of small animals, including some gazelles, coming to drink.

"Well, that will do for a starter," announced Joe, as they neared the train.

"Pretty good, too," declared Blake. "But when we get away from the railroad and into the real jungle, we'll do better."

The telegraph line had been repaired, and orders to proceed having been received they started off once more. Nothing more of interest occurred that day, though on the next the boys managed to get a few views of a clumsy rhinoceros, as it waddled along the track for some distance. The engine was stopped to enable the boys to get the pictures they desired. The rhino seemed undecided about charging, but finally made up his mind not to.

On another occasion, when they had to stop for some slight repairs to the engine, the boys went off into the jungle on the chance of filming some lions, as tracks were seen near the rails. But they had no success.

In due time they reached Port Florence, on Victoria Nyanza, having made some very good films, but hoping to make much better ones.

"And now we're really on what is to us the most important part of our journey," said Mr. Duncan to the boys. "Once we are across the lake, we will be far from civilization, in the heart of the jungle, and there is where we expect to find Jessie."

"And we will find her, too!" declared Joe, with conviction.

"What about our safari?" asked Blake. "Are we going to get our natives here?"

"I'll see about that," said Sergeant Hotchkiss.

They remained at Port Florence several days, and on the morning of the fourth they heard confused sounds outside of their stopping place.

"What's that?" cried Joe, as he got up to look.

"Sounds like a minstrel chorus," said Blake.

"It's our native party!" cried his chum. "Look!"

As they peered from their window they saw a score of almost naked savages—black as coals—with only blankets on, their ears heavy with all sorts of ornaments, from empty tin cans to big bones, sticking in the lobes, their hair plastered with mud, carrying long spears, or sticks, and all going through a sort of dance, chanting the while in a strange tongue.

"For the love of cats, what is that?" cried C. C., as he joined the boys. "Have they come to eat us? Are they cannibals?"

"Indeed they are not," said Mr. Hotchkiss, who entered the room at that moment. "Those are the porters I have engaged to take us and our baggage into the interior of the jungle. They will form our expedition. In Africa you can't get along without them. They are all fine fellows, I assure you, and faithful. You can trust them with your lives."

"Well, they don't look so," spoke C. C., as he pointed to one gigantic black, who looked particularly hideous with the skull of a hyena fastened on top of his head.

"He sure is the limit," agreed Joe.

"And his name is Happy One," said the sergeant. "Come down, and I'll introduce you to them in form."

"And are they the natives who are to lead me to my daughter?" asked Mr. Duncan.

"They are," said the sergeant, gravely. "And if they can't do it, no one can."

"But they will!" cried C. C., in his new, jolly manner. "We'll find her, all right!"

CHAPTER X
AT A BIG RISK

JOE AND BLAKE LOOKED out on the queer throng of native porters. The Africans seemed a motley lot with which to venture into the interior of the jungle, far away from other white men, and entirely out of reach of such British law and force as ruled in that part of the big continent.

"Some of them positively look as though they would enjoy doing a war dance around us," suggested Blake.

"That's right," agreed his chum. "And yet I suppose Sergeant Hotchkiss knows his business. He wouldn't hire dangerous characters."

"Indeed no," put in Mr. Duncan. "I warned him to be careful in the selection of our porters, and he assured me he would only get such as had been on safari before. I trust he has done so."

"He seems to know some of them, at any rate," said C. C., for the former Boer soldier had gone out to the black men, leaving his employers to follow. "He's talking and laughing with them," went on the actor, "and they seem jolly enough. Look at Happy One, as he is called—the chap with the hyena skull on his head. He's doing a regular two-step."

"And lots of them are singing," observed Blake, as the notes of a strange and rather weird chant came to them.

"By Jove, I know what I'm going to do," declared Joe.

"What?" asked his chum.

"I'm going to make some moving pictures of them. They will go well as a sort of introduction to the views of wild animals we may get."

Blake agreed with this, and while Mr. Duncan was being formally presented to the porters as the ostensible head of the safari (it being decided to do this rather than have the boys pose as the proprietors) the lads got their moving picture machine ready.

And as the big black men, with their fantastic dress and queer ornaments, paraded around Mr. Duncan, singing (as he learned later) his praises as one who would "give much meat," the boys filmed the odd sight.

"Queer they don't seem to mind it a bit," said Blake, as some of the blacks actually posed before the lens.

"Oh, most of them have been on safari before," explained the sergeant, as he heard this. "They have been with white men, some of whom hunted, while others took pictures, and, though the camera is much of a mystery to them, they don't mind it in the least. But what do you think of them?"

"An odd lot," was Joe's opinion, as he ceased grinding at the handle of the camera.

"Can you trust them?" asked Blake.

"I think so," said the former soldier. "Of course, human nature is the same the world over. Some of the men are what are called 'mission' boys—that is, they have been Christianized, after a fashion. They are very good. The others can also be trusted, I think."

"And do they realize that we may come to a clash with the tribesmen who may have my daughter?" asked Mr. Duncan.

"I have explained," said the sergeant, "that there may be a fight."

"What did they say?" asked the anxious father.

"They gave the best answer possible. They sharpened their spears, and looked to their shields."

"Then it's all right," said Mr. Duncan, in relieved tones. "We can't get Jessie all alone—we white men. We will have to depend on the natives we take with us. But are we ready to march, Mr. Hotchkiss?"

"Yes, we'll go aboard the steamer, and on arrival at Entebbe we'll trek into the jungle. Are you ready to go?"

"Have we all our supplies?" asked C. C. "I don't want to starve—oh, of course we won't starve!" he added, hastily. "I am getting into my old habits," and he laughed.

"Everything is in readiness," answered the sergeant, who had looked after all the details. "I'll give the word now, the porters will be assigned each to his load, and we will go aboard. We will start across the Victoria Nyanza in about an hour."

Then began a busy time. Each porter was to carry a load of about sixty pounds. This is found to be as much as a man can march with, day after day, often without water or food, and over all sorts of country.

The packs were made up of various objects—food, supplies of different kinds, ammunition for the rifles and revolvers, some medicines, and, of course, the cameras and films.

Tents were carried, to afford shelter at night, for though it is stiflingly hot during the African day, the nights, with their heavy dews, are very cold. And indeed, in the higher parts of the continent, the climate is as cool and healthful as any part of the United States. Often it is possible to camp in sight of mountains whose summits are covered with perpetual snow.

Under the direction of Sergeant Hotchkiss, order was brought out of chaos. The porters were checked off and given their place in line, though the actual march would not begin until after Entebbe was reached. But it was desired to have all in readiness to avoid confusion later.

"Happy One," who spoke considerable English, was made the head porter, and it was easy to see that the selection pleased him. The others, too, seemed to take to him, and it was hoped there would be no trouble.

There were few passengers on the steamer by which our friends were to make the trip across the northern part of the lake.

"It doesn't seem as if we were in the heart of Africa," remarked Blake, on the afternoon of embarking. "Here we are, on a fairly comfortable steamer, on a big lake, and with almost unknown land all about us. Right in the heart of what was unknown entirely not many years ago. Think of it, Joe!"

"I am thinking of it, Blake," was the answer, "but while it is strange, still we've been in so many odd places of late that this doesn't seem to impress me as it ought."

"I suppose you're thinking of Jessie," said his chum, in a low voice.

"Yes; that's it. If we were only on a pleasure or business journey, intending only to get views of wild animals, I might think differently. But I can't get over thinking of my little sister, with her missionary friends, in the hands of savages—perhaps in the midst of some wild jungle!"

"It is tough, Joe. But don't give up hope yet. Why, even C. C. goes ahead of you these days. He's jolly."

"I know he is, and I mustn't give way to my fears," went on Joe. "I won't—that's all! Now let's enjoy this view."

They were sailing over one of the largest lakes of Africa. Their baggage had been put away, and the native porters, in their section of the craft, were devoting themselves to their pastimes. Mr. Duncan kept rather to himself, or talked with the sergeant, and the boys and Mr. Piper walked about, looking sometimes at the Africans at their simple games, at the engines of the boat, or gazing across the stretch of waters.

"There doesn't seem to be much chance for pictures here," remarked Joe, when they had been traveling for a day or two. "I wish we could film something."

He and his chum had a chance not long after that, when the steamer put in at a small port to leave some goods for an Englishman who had started an ostrich ranch there. It was in rather a lonely spot. There was no dock for the steamer, and the goods had to be taken ashore in small boats.

"This is going to take some time," said Mr. Hotchkiss, after a talk with the captain, "and, if you boys want to go ashore, you are at liberty to borrow a boat. You may see something worth filming, as you call it."

"I wonder if we could get a rhino?" asked Joe.

"I don't believe you'll find any in this locality," answered the former soldier; "but, of course, Africa is a strange place. You may stir up game when you least expect it."

"Let's try," suggested Joe, and his chum agreed.

"I'll go along, and see if I can get a shot at anything," said C. C. "You may need my services."

They were soon rowing toward shore in one of the small boats of the steamer, with the moving picture camera in the bow ready for instant use.

They soon found where a small stream, flowing into the lake, gave them a chance to get off the main body of water.

"Let's try that," suggested Joe. "It's too open here to get anything. Let's go where it's wilder."

"It's wild enough here!" exclaimed Blake, a little later, when they were rowing along, hardly able to move from the number of lily pads on the surface of the stream. The lilies themselves, great yellow and white blossoms, were all about, amid the broad green leaves, on top of which stepped peculiar birds, with long claws, seemingly made for traveling on the pads. The edges of the stream were lost in a mass of tall papyrus, the plants from which the ancients made paper.

"Yes, it is wild," agreed Joe, "but I don't see anything to make pictures of, and—"

But he did not finish. He was interrupted by a sort of coughing groan just ahead of them. There was a stir among the lily pads. The water swirled, and up from it heaved a black, bulky body.

"What's that?" cried Blake, in some alarm.

"A hippopotamus!" cried Joe. "Hurray! Something to film at last! Row us toward it, if you don't mind, C. C."

"It's taking a big risk," said the actor, solemnly. "If he rushes us we won't have much chance!"

"We'll take it," decided Joe. "Put us closer."

"Yes, do," urged Blake, and the comedian, looking to see that his heavy gun was in readiness, bent to the oars. Joe stood ready to turn the camera handle.

At that moment the hippopotamus, which had only partly risen from the stream, heaved up, and there confronted the boys an enormous mouth, wide open, showing a big expanse of red, with long and cruel-looking teeth lining it.

Then, with another grunt, the hippo moved directly toward the boat, while the camera began clicking.

CHAPTER XI
"FORWARD!"

"LET'S GET OUT OF this!" cried Mr. Piper. "He'll crush this boat with one bite!"

"I guess you're right," agreed Joe. "Let's row to shore, Blake. I've heard they can't go very fast on land!"

"Maybe we can scare him off!" suggested the other. Blake was not fool-hardy, but he really did not understand the danger of the hippo as the actor-hunter did. Besides, he wanted to get some fine films, and this was a rare chance. He had been in many dangerous places before, but never such as this. He totally underestimated the terrible power and the unreasoning anger of the huge beast they had come upon.

"There!" cried Blake; "he's dived! I told you it would be all right! He's afraid of us!"

"Don't you believe it!" shouted C. C., as he laid aside the gun he had caught up, and began to labor with the oars, forcing the boat toward the papyrus-lined shore of the sluggish stream. "He's going to come up under the boat if he can, upset us, and take us all in at one bite! I know hippos!"

But Joe, imbued with something of the reckless courage displayed by his chum, held his place at the moving picture machine, as did Blake. Together they revolved the handle, making views of the swirling waters where the hippo had disappeared—bubbles, foam and little swirling eddys showing where the big river-horse had sunk.

"What do you think, Joe?" asked Blake. "Shall we chance it any longer?"

"I think so. He doesn't seem as bad as C. C. thinks he is. Anyhow, he went down without attacking us, and he may pass us up altogether. If he does, we'll get him running away, and that will make another good part of the film. Let's stick!"

"That's what I say. It isn't every day we get a chance like this. If we had—"

Once more Blake was interrupted in what he started to say by the action of the clumsy beast, yet which could move with considerable speed in the water in spite of its vast bulk.

There was a sinuous motion to the lily pads, stems and flowers. They parted and something arose amid them.

"Here he is again!" cried Blake.

"Yes, and he means business, too!" yelled Joe. "C. C., it's up to you to do something! We haven't time to row ashore."

This was very evident, for the hippo had, this time, risen so close to the boat that the boys thought they could feel his hot breath. The monstrous mouth was wide open, and the red throat, looking like some immense flannel bag, seemed yawning for them. The hippo could easily have crushed the boat amidships, and there was no time to back water.

"Shoot! Shoot!" yelled Joe.

"I guess I'll have to!" cried C. C. Piper; "but it's a last hope. I can't stop him at such short range!"

He dropped the oars and caught up the heavy elephant gun. Even in this excitement Blake continued to grind away at the camera, getting some views at close range. Then, thinking that the boat would be crushed, and wishing to save the machine and the rare films if possible, he caught up the apparatus and fled to the stern, leaving the actor-hunter a clear view.

With coughs, grunts and groans of protest that his river home had thus been invaded, the hippo swam on. Now and then he closed the enormous jaws with a crunching sound, and at such times the lower jaws went under water, and when it was closed the water splashed out on both sides in miniature fountains.

"Shoot, if you're going to, C. C.!" yelled Joe.

"Here goes for a slim chance!" cried Mr. Piper.

At that moment the big beast again opened wide his jaws. He was but a few feet from the boat now, and the wave of his advance caused the craft to rock dangerously.

Aiming directly down the big red throat, C. C. fired. The report of the heavy gun at such close quarters almost deafened the boys, and the recoil nearly tossed the hunter overboard. But he maintained his balance.

Joe and Blake eagerly looked where the hippo had been. There was no need of waiting for the smoke to clear away, as the actor-hunter was using nitro cartridges, which were smokeless.

"He's gone!" shouted Joe.

"He sank at the shot!" cried Blake.

"I guess I did tickle his throat some," remarked Mr. Piper, grimly. "That was a heavy bullet, and it must have gone clear through him."

"I wonder if you killed him?" spoke Joe. "Jove! if you did—at one shot. Let's see if he's a goner."

"No use to wait," said Mr. Piper. "A hippo, when shot, whether mortally or not, sinks immediately. If it is dead it won't float for nearly a day, and we can't stay here that long. If he's only wounded he'll swim off under water and come up, the land knows where. No, we're lucky to be rid of him so easily. I never thought I could stop him at such short range, but the bullet must have gone in a tender spot."

"Well, we got some dandy pictures," spoke Blake, fervently.

"That's what," agreed Joe.

A distant whistle was heard, echoing faintly over the sluggish river.

"That's the steamer calling us, I guess," said Mr. Piper. "Let's get back."

Slowly they rowed out into the main lake, well satisfied with their adventure, and, now that the danger was over, almost forgetting it.

"Don't tell Dad all about it," suggested Joe to his chum. "He may think it was worse than it really was, and not let us go out again. He doesn't know that we've been used to taking chances; Blake, and he still thinks, in a way, that I'm only a little chap. Do you see?"

"Yes," agreed his chum. "We won't make him worry any."

But if Mr. Duncan did not understand the danger of filming a hippo at the charge, Sergeant Hotchkiss did, and he warned the boys, in private, to be very careful.

The landing of the freight was accomplished, and once more the trip across the lake was begun. Ordinarily this voyage, from Port Florence to Entebbe, takes but twenty-four hours, but the steamer carrying our friends was a slow one, and in addition had to make many stops. Then, too, something happened to the engine once or twice, and there were long delays for repairs. So that they were three days making the passage.

Eventually, however, Entebbe was reached. This was quite a large town, where many English and other white residents lived. Many marks of civilization were observed, there being even a private auto garage, while a number of bicyclists were seen on the streets.

"Think of that—in Africa!" cried Joe.

"I'll be looking for a sign of Broadway and Forty-second street soon," said Blake.

"Oh, Africa isn't half so uncivilized as it was," said Sergeant Hotchkiss; "and yet don't go away with the notion that this town is far removed from the jungle. It isn't. Why, on the outskirts the wild animals come in. Herds of zebras often spoil the fruit trees, and flower and vegetable beds. And there is danger from other beasts, too. Often people are attacked going from one house to another at night, and I have heard it said that on going out to spend the evening the men always take guns. They might have to use it on a rhino or something coming home."

"Really?" asked Mr. Duncan.

"That's a fact," the sergeant assured him, and, to my readers, I might add that all the essential facts given in this book, both as regards the wild animal life of Africa, as well as the making of moving pictures, are true, and can be verified by those who care to do so.

In the native part of Entebbe dwelt the young King of Uganda, and the boys had a chance to take some moving pictures of him and his court, some of the attendants at which had adopted European dress, while the others wore nothing but a blanket. Even the king was still enough of a barbarian to delight in the beating of many drums, though he had an English tutor.

"This is too civilized for us," remarked Blake one day, when they had been in Entebbe about a week making further arrangements to go into the interior. "Look at 'em playing tennis, Joe," and he pointed to a court where some of the English residents were enjoying a game.

"That's right, Blake. We ought to be in the jungle. But I guess we're almost ready to trek. Dad is getting impatient."

"We leave tomorrow, boys," announced Sergeant Hotchkiss that night. "I have all the supplies we need now. I have engaged a few more porters, gotten some more ammunition, and we can now head for Kargos. What we'll find there, of course, I don't know," and he looked serious.

"The best I hope for," said Mr. Duncan, "is to get some trace of my daughter. If the missionary station is wholly destroyed there may still be some clue that will help us get on the right trail. Or some of the natives, some who had begun to learn Christianity, may still be about and can aid us."

"I hope so," murmured Blake, and Joe sighed as he nodded his head in agreement.

They had made inquiries, and learned that Kargos was a native settlement about five days' march from Entebbe, in a dense part of the jungle. It was some distance back from the lake, and inhabited by several fierce and warlike tribes. But aside from the news that the mission station had been destroyed by a raiding party of blacks, no particulars could be learned. The whites—Mr. and Mrs. Brown, and their assistant, Jessie Duncan—seemed to have completely disappeared. Whether they had been killed, or were taken captive, no one knew, though all hoped for the latter alternative.

The last arrangements were made. The porters' burdens were packed anew, the last supplies were bought, guns and ammunition looked to, and, one sunny morning, the word to start was given.

Horses had been provided for the whites, and one or two mules carried the heavier burdens; but all would have to accommodate their pace to the march of the porters. However, these men of iron frame and constitution could cover many miles in a day.

Quite a number of the residents of Entebbe came to see the expedition start, as word of its object had leaked out. There was much sympathy expressed for Joe and his father, and all hoped they would find Jessie.

"All ready?" cried Sergeant Hotchkiss, as he looked over the line of porters with their loads on their heads.

"Ready!" cried Happy One, the leader, as he danced about, his fantastic headdress of a hyena's skull bobbing up and down. He had removed it from his crown, as it did not fit in with the plan of carrying a burden, and it was suspended about his neck by a thong.

"Ready!" cried Mr. Duncan.

"Forward, then!" exclaimed the sergeant, and to the weird cries of the Africans, accompanied by the beating of the tom-toms some carried, the party started into the jungle.

CHAPTER XII
AT THE BURNED STATION

"WELL, JOE, HOW DO you like it?"

"I don't know, Blake. It's a heap-sight different from camping out on our Western plains."

"I should say so!" exclaimed C. C. Piper. "If there's one inch of me that hasn't been bitten by some of these ticks, I'd like someone to point it out. I know I'll never get back alive to—"

"Hold on there!" cried Blake, with a laugh, "I thought you'd given up all that sort of thing, since coming to Africa."

"So I have," answered the hunter-actor. "I forgot myself for a moment. At the same time, those ticks do bite; but I suppose it had better be them than a hippo," and he proceeded to apply some healing lotion to the bites of the insects that make life in Africa a burden to man and beast, not even the mighty lion, nor the thick-skinned rhinoceros, escaping.

"I never thought the mosquitoes would be so bad," came from the tent where Mr. Duncan was sleeping—or, rather, trying to sleep. "There must be a hole in my mosquito canopy," he went on.

"Do as I once read of an Irishman doing," suggested Sergeant Hotchkiss.

"How was that?" asked Mr. Piper.

"Why, the Irishman put up at a hotel in some part of Jersey, where the mosquitoes were very bad," went on the former Boer soldier. "He was shown to his room, and found a mosquito netting over the bed. He didn't know exactly what it was for, but he managed to solve the problem to his own satisfaction at least. In the morning the hotel clerk asked him how he slept, also inquiring if the mosquitoes bothered him very much.

"The Irishman said they did, until he had an inspiration. He said he tore a hole in the 'fishnet' over his bed.

"'Sure and all the mosquitoes went in that,' he said, 'and I just laid down on the floor, after closin' up the hole, with them all inside, and slept in peace and quietness.'"

"That's pretty good," remarked Mr. Duncan, "but I don't believe African mosquitoes are like that."

It was their third day out, and they had traveled over a considerable stretch of country. The porters were fresh, and had made good time. Mr. Piper was lucky enough to shoot a big eland, and this furnished meat, which the white travelers were almost as glad to partake of as were the blacks.

The boys had tried several times to get moving pictures of some of the herds of wildebeest or hartebeest, a species of antelope, and also the numerous gazelles, the Thompson variety, known locally as "Tommy's," and also the Grant. But they had been unsuccessful from various causes. Sometimes, just as they got ready to begin grinding away at the film, having placed the camera at some water hole, or stream where game came to drink, the clicking would frighten the timid creatures away.

Or the deer would scent some animal that they dreaded—a lion or leopard, and would gallop off before Joe or Blake could get the desired films.

Then, if they waited for the more powerful animals to appear, something might frighten them off, and so the opportunity would be lost.

"But we'll get 'em yet," said Joe. "I'd rather get some of the wilder or bigger animals, if we could, instead of these deer-like creatures, anyhow."

"Oh, we'll get 'em all in time," declared his chum.

And so they had traveled on, the expedition making good time. During the terrible heat of midday, almost on the equator as they were, they rested in shade if they could find it, or under their tents. At night they would seek out some spot near water, tether their animals, raise the canvas shelters, and have supper, dining on the provisions they had brought with them, or on what game Mr. Piper or the sergeant shot.

Occasionally the boys themselves, under the guidance of the former soldier, would go out and try their luck at providing the larder with something substantial. And often they were lucky, for the country abounded in game.

Then, when the porters came back laden with meat, there would be general rejoicing, Happy One leading the chant in honor of the white men and boys.

And now they had come again to a night camp. Fires had been lighted in several places, about which squatted the blacks, with their scanty blankets. But they did not mind the ticks and mosquitoes, as long as they were warm and well fed.

"A strange sight," murmured C. C., as he looked from the tent where all the whites slept, out on the surrounding camp fires. The flames played on the strongly-marked features of the blacks, throwing them into bold relief. Happy One, who had resumed his hyena skull headpiece on getting rid of his burden, went from place to place, here starting a weird song, there pausing to tell some story of the ancient days.

The smell of cooking was in the air, for the African porters never seemed to tire of eating. Even as they sang they roasted strips of meat on slender sticks at the blazes.

"It sure is strange," agreed Blake, as he looked on the scene. "Getting the films of the Indians was nothing to this."

"But we haven't got many films as yet," said Joe.

"No, but we will," said his chum. "We will soon be at Kargos, and then—"

"Then we may find some trace of Sister Jessie," said Joe, in a low voice. "I only hope we do."

They talked for some time longer, and then turned over and tried to go to sleep. It was not easy work. Their surroundings were strange, and they were not as comfortable as they might have been, though they had brought all the conveniences they could with them.

Even at that, with the chattering of baboons in the distance, the night-noises of the wild fowl and the birds, the occasional grunt of a hippo or the louder noise of the rhino, like some locomotive whistling and blowing off steam at the same time, there was enough disturbance to keep even a bigger camp awake.

Then, when they did drop off into a doze, there came a sudden alarm. From afar sounded a noise like thunder. It rumbled and roared, and the boys sat up on their collapsible cots.

"What is it?" cried Joe.

"A storm," answered his chum.

"Lions!" exclaimed Sergeant Hotchkiss, who had caught the words of the frightened porters.

They all turned out with their guns, while the fires blazed brightly from the wood thrown on by the natives. But the noise died off in the distance, and the beasts that are called the "kings" of the jungle sought some other spot to make their nightly kill.

"Oh, for a chance to take a picture of the lions!" sighed Joe, as he again sought his bed.

"We'll get it yet," said Blake, as he, too, turned in.

The next day broke hot and dry. They had been subject to a number of thunder storms, in which the vividness of the lightning and the terrific explosions of heaven's artillery they had never seen nor heard equaled, but now there seemed to come a period of calm, and they traveled onward amid intense heat.

It was hard work, but the porters, under the "jollying" of Happy One, did not seem to mind it. C. C., too, seemed to retain his good spirits and made no direful predictions.

But Mr. Duncan, no less than Joe and Blake, was anxious to get to the place where, according to reports, his daughter had last been. They questioned many native tribes, as they went along, and were told that the mission station was still many miles farther along.

"And when we get there, what will we find?" asked Joe, and there was anxiety in his tone.

"Maybe not as bad as we have heard," said Blake, encouragingly.

And so they traveled on. Lucky it was that C. C. and Sergeant Hotchkiss were along, for on them devolved the work of keeping the camp in meat. The boys did their best, but they had not had the experience, nor the practice in bringing down big game. But the former soldier and the actor-hunter were sharp on the trail, and brought down many a lusty buck of the antelope species, occasionally getting a giraffe, or some smaller animal good for food. Everything was grist that came to the mill of the Africans, though the whites were more fastidious. Though even with the most unprepossessing animals there were some parts good for food.

"Well, I wonder what we'll strike today?" spoke Joe, on the second day's trek after their night when the mosquitoes and ticks had been so troublesome.

"More moving pictures, I hope," said his chum.

That day they had been lucky enough to film a herd of giraffes feeding on the tops of some tall trees. The two lads had managed to creep up close under cover, and, setting their cameras, had snapped the tall, but in a way graceful, creatures as they ate. There was no desire to shoot them, but some noise gave the alarm, and away they went over the plain at an ungainly gallop, their tails twisting about in the queerest fashion.

"We are getting near the village where my sister was," went on Joe, in a low voice. "Happy One, according to the sergeant, said that by noon we would make it. I wonder what we'll find there. If we can only pick up some clue—"

"Of course we will," put in C. C., cheerfully.

A little later there came a shout from the porters who were in the lead. There appeared to be considerable excitement, and at first the boys thought something had happened.

"An attack by some wild animal!" cried Joe.

"A lion, maybe," added Blake. "Get the camera ready."

"That isn't an alarm," said Sergeant Hotchkiss, quietly.

"What is it, then?" asked Mr. Duncan.

"They are singing a song of lament—of sorrow," was the answer.

A chill struck to the hearts of the boys, as they pushed forward. What would they see?

"It must be the station where—where Jessie was," said Mr. Duncan, bro-kenly. "If there are any of the mission people left they may be able to—"

But he did not finish. Accompanied by the boys he made a turn in the trail which brought him to the little clearing where the mission had been. But the station was gone.

It had been destroyed, and nothing but a fire-blackened area marked where it had stood. There were the ruins of the buildings, and of the charred huts occupied by the natives from whom an attempt had been made to lift the darkness of ignorance. All was gone! The little church was burned—nothing but a pile of charred timbers. The raiders had done their work well.

The song of the African porters seemed to become more and more melan-choly. They felt for their white employers, for the story of the search for the daughter of Mr. Duncan was known to all.

"Nothing left!" exclaimed Mr. Duncan, and he placed his hand on Joe's shoulder. "Not a trace. Oh, my poor Jessie!"

There was silence for a moment, and then C. C. Piper, who had gone for-ward, uttered a cry—a cry of joy, it seemed.

"What is it?" asked Blake, eagerly. "Have you a clue?"

"I think I have, and a good one, too!" replied the actor-hunter.

CHAPTER XIII
THE LION HUNT

CROWDING AROUND MR. PIPER they all tried at once to look at what he had picked up. It was something covered with dust and ashes—something swollen with the rains that had fallen—a strange, misshapen thing, that seemed to be a book, and yet which might have been almost anything.

"What is it?" cried Joe.

"Is it any message from my daughter?" demanded the former sailor, as with trembling hands he reached for it.

"It's a small Bible," said C. C., as he examined it. "But there is some writing on the first page."

Blake, feeling that this was too sacred a moment for him to intrude, held back, as did Sergeant Hotchkiss. Joe and his father took the little book, which had almost lost semblance to itself.

"It is a Bible," spoke Joe, softly.

"And here is Jessie's name in it," went on Mr. Duncan, as he scanned the writing on the first page. "It is a gift from Mr. and Mrs. Brown. Oh, how glad I am that I have this memento of my little girl. If only—"

"There's more writing there, Dad!" exclaimed Joe, as he looked over his father's shoulder. "And it's in a different hand from the other. Could Jessie have written that?"

Anxiously Mr. Duncan scanned it. Then he cried out:

"I never saw her writing, but this seems to be hers. She appears to have written a message. Blake, your eyes are better than mine. See if you can make anything of this," and he handed over the book. No wonder his eyes were dim—the tears made them so.

Eagerly Blake scanned the title page of the little Bible, blackened by fire and smoke and soaked with rain. He could trace some lines, but they were so faint—

"Try this!" exclaimed C. C., holding out a pocket reading glass. "It will magnify the lines."

Once more Blake looked.

"It is a message," he said. "It seems to have been written in a hurry, and not with ink. It looks more like ashes and water mixed."

"I have it!" interrupted Joe. "My sister was surprised, as were the others, by the raid. She only had time to leave a hasty message, and, there being no ink, she dipped a sharp stick in a mixture of water and ashes, and left her message that way."

"It does seem so," admitted Sergeant Hotchkiss. "Can you read it, Blake?"

Slowly Blake spelled out the scrawled words:

"'To—any—'" he began, "'to any who come—after. We have—been carried away by the natives—to the—' It looks like 'south,'" said Blake. "It's so blurred."

"That's 'south,'" was Joe's opinion, as he looked over his chum's shoulder. "They took 'em south."

"'We have been carried off to the south,'" read Blake. "'Help us if you can. I think they mean to hold us for ransom.'"

"Thank the dear Lord for that!" breathed Mr. Duncan. "Now let's start at once. Off to the south, to rescue my daughter! Sergeant, ask these natives what they know of the tribes south. Are they friendly? Will they give up Jessie? I'll spend my last dollar for her recovery!"

The sergeant paused a moment.

"We must go slow," he said. "I must think about this. I will have a talk with Happy One. He is a wise old native."

Mr. Duncan was all for starting off at once, but the others persuaded him to wait and so make a better and more detailed plan. Accordingly camp was made near the burned missionary station.

It was evident that the friendly natives at the little village, and the missionaries, had been surprised by the warlike Africans. Whether any had been killed could only be guessed at. Certainly the station had been pillaged, and some of the inmates, if not all, had been carried off. The Bible hastily written in and tossed aside by Jessie, in the hope that someone would find it, was evidence enough.

And the trail seemingly led south, according to her clue, though when Happy One was appealed to he declared that only friendly natives dwelt there—natives who were inclined to Christianity, and who would never think of raiding a mission.

"But some of the more warlike ones may have come from there," insisted Mr. Duncan. "I think we should search to the south."

And so, the next morning, in spite of the advice of Happy One, they trekked south. It was useless to look for clues, but there seemed to be a sort of rough trail leading from the station to the southward, and this was taken.

They were three days on the march—days fraught with danger and discomfort, for part of the way lay through a swamp which was too large to go around. Once some of the porters sank to their hips, and only prompt work saved them and their precious loads. For the expedition was now getting far from all sources of supplies, and everything they had with them was of vital necessity.

Again they stirred up a herd of buffalo, which were on the point of charging, and only a fusillade of shots drove them away.

On this occasion Blake and Joe tried for some moving pictures, but, though they got out their cameras as soon as the herd was turned aside, it was too late, and only some unsatisfactory films were obtained.

Another time, at dusk, they disturbed a couple of the prehensile-lip rhinoceroses, who blindly charged, though our friends had no intention of harming them.

C. C. Piper had to do some quick shooting then. He killed one of the queer beasts and wounded another, and the slain one made the natives happy, for they were short of meat.

But on one occasion the boys did get a series of fine pictures. This was at a water hole, in the midst of a plain surrounded by a growth of timber which gave them a screen. They ascended a tree with their camera, and after a long wait they succeeded in filming a number of baboons as they came to drink. Then came a couple of giraffes, which spread their tall front legs in ungainly fashion in order to bring their heads close enough to sip the water in the low pool.

Afterward came a family of elephants, one a little one, and they drank their fill, the baboons retiring a safe distance, being the weaker animals, though this species is dangerous in the extreme. With their terrible teeth and their claws they are, in small droves, a match for many animals—but not the elephant.

"A good day's work!" exclaimed Joe, when they came away from the water hole.

"Some dandy films!" was Blake's opinion. "And, best of all, we didn't have to go out of our way to get them," for they were still traveling south on the trail of the kidnapped missionaries.

There had been some indications of the passage of a body of natives in that direction. Whether or not they had with them Jessie and the other white captives was a matter of conjecture. Still Joe and his father had hopes. They would not give up until the last.

The march was resumed after the stop at the water hole, where enough game was killed to last for several days. They came to a stream of water, where a number of antelopes were seen, and Joe and Blake were fortunate enough to get a very rare picture—a view of two noble Koodoo bucks having a battle royal. So interested were the animals themselves in the outcome that they never noticed the moving picture boys, who stood in plain view, in a clearing, making films. Nor did the others in the herd take the alarm until the fight was over and one of the bucks vanquished.

Then some movement on the part of Blake or Joe startled them, and they were off at a gallop, leaving the injured buck on the ground. But his flesh made good food for the black porters.

The journey was ever onward, and several days after the finding of the Bible, Happy One, who was in the lead, suddenly threw down his bundle, readjusted his hyena headdress, and began brandishing his spear.

"What is it?" asked Blake in some alarm.

"Simba! Simba!" cried Happy One.

"He says lion," interpreted the sergeant.

"A lion!" cried C. C. "If that's the case—" and he made a quick motion toward his gun.

"Oh, there's no lion about to charge," said Mr. Hotchkiss, hastily. "Probably Happy One has sighted a party of African hunters after a lion. There is no beast the blacks fear so much as the simba, or lion, and they always rejoice when one is about to be killed. I think you'll find that to be the case."

There was a confused shouting up front. Many of the porters got rid of their loads, and began dancing about. The whites pushed forward and beheld a curious sight.

Marching toward them was a band of African hunters, each one carrying a big spear with a head several feet long, of soft iron, sharpened to a razor-like edge. The butt of the spears, too, was partly of iron, only the middle being of wood, and the natives all carried ox-hide shields.

They were tall and straight, these savages, fierce and fearless-looking; true lion hunters. And, as they advanced, they broke into a chant.

"That's it!" cried the sergeant. "It's a lion hunt, all right. Boys, you're in luck! Get your cameras ready, and you'll see a rare sight—lions hunted by means of spears and shields!"

"Good!" cried Blake, while Joe hurried back toward the mule that carried the moving picture outfits.

CHAPTER XIV
THE WRONG TRAIL

"WHAT'S IT ALL ABOUT?" asked Mr. Duncan. "I don't exactly understand, sergeant. Is there to be a lion hunt here?"

"That's about it, Mr. Duncan," answered the former soldier. "That is, not exactly here, but in this vicinity. These are some Masai warriors out on a hunt. Probably their village is near here, and there may have been trouble with lions. I'll have a talk with them, and we'll find out. But if they stir up one of the beasts you will sure see some great fighting, my word!" and he lapsed into his English idiom.

"But will they hunt the lion with just those spears?" asked C. C. Piper, wonderingly. "No guns, no revolvers for work at close quarters? I say, now. I think we ought to offer them the use of a gun or two."

"They'd feel insulted if you did," said Mr. Hotchkiss. "It is their boast that they can kill lions with only their spears, with their shields for defense. They would scorn to use a gun. But we'll soon see what's up. Got your cameras ready, boys?"

"We will have, soon," replied Blake.

"This doesn't look much like lion country," spoke Joe.

"You never can tell," answered the sergeant.

By this time the advancing warriors, who wore only loin cloths, had come to a halt at the sight of the safari. They were a bold and savage-looking lot of men, and the absence of any women or children betokened that they were bent on desperate business.

"Maybe they're on the warpath," suggested Mr. Duncan. "Can it be that savages, such as these, have carried off my little daughter?"

"I hardly believe so," answered the sergeant. "Certainly this particular tribe did not, for they don't do such things. It is more likely some of the lower class African races. In fact, according to our information, none of the Masai were involved in the kidnapping. But they want a parley, I see."

The lion hunters had halted, and one, seemingly the chief, now advanced. There was nothing hostile in their actions, for doubtless the sight of the native porters, and hearing the marching songs they sung, told them that our friends were on a peaceful errand.

But, as one's life in Africa depends on the attitude of not only beasts, but savage men, it is best to take no chances. The chief of the lion hunters came forward and began to talk in a deep, almost booming voice. He used simple but effective gestures, and really seemed quite a dignified savage.

"You forget that he hasn't many clothes on, when you hear him talk," said Joe.

"That's right," agreed Blake; "I wonder what he is saying? Happy One seems to understand him."

This was so, and in a few moments the head porter and the chief lion hunter were in a friendly conversation. Then Sergeant Hotchkiss took part in it, as he understood some of the Masai language, and presently the former soldier said:

"It's just as I expected. They are out on the trail of a pair of lions that have carried off several of their cattle, and have injured some of their tribe. They invite us to go along, but they expressly stipulate that no guns are to be used."

"Not even if there is danger of the lion attacking them?" C. C. wanted to know.

"Not even then," insisted Mr. Hotchkiss. "They say they can take care of the lion with their spears; and they can, too. My word! I've seen 'em. I have told them the boys want some moving pictures of it, and they are willing. Now trail along. Of course, if you find yourselves in danger from a lion, don't hesitate to shoot, but don't even to save a native's life—that is, one of the Masai natives—don't fire. They would never forgive you if you did."

He said something to the Masai chief, who, in turn, addressed his men. The latter called out what seemed to be a salute to the white men, and the latter's porters answered. Then they started off.

Leaving their property in charge of the native porters, one and all of whom refused to come on the lion hunt, Joe and Blake, with the sergeant and Mr. Piper, started after the warriors. Mr. Duncan elected to stay with the baggage.

"Better take these with you," said C. C., to the boys, as they started off with their cameras, for each had one of the moving picture machines.

"What?" asked Blake.

"A heavy revolver. In case of the worst, if the lion comes at you, and those fellows don't stop him with their spears, you may need it."

"That's right," agreed Joe.

They slipped the weapons into their pockets and started off, eager to see what would happen. Their way soon lay across a plain of rather high grass.

The hunters were strung out in a long line, covering a wide area, for the lion might be come upon at any time now.

After a few miles of this progress, during which there were several false alarms, they came to a small valley. Tall rushes and grass grew in the centre, with here and there thorn trees of no great height.

The head hunter called out something, and his men replied in a fierce chorus.

"He says," translated the sergeant, "that here, if anywhere, we'll stir up a lion."

"Good!" cried Blake.

The line of warriors advanced. They were rather silent now, wary and cautious, with their spears and shields in readiness. The boys were on the alert.

Suddenly came another shout, and the blacks broke into a run.

"Simba! Simba!" was the cry.

"A lion!" shouted the sergeant.

And there, just ahead of them, sprang up a great tawny beast with a shaggy mane—a yellow terror of the jungle—a full grown, male lion.

The hunters broke into a joyous shout, spreading out fanwise. The lion leaped ahead, intent on escaping, for well he must have known the fate in store for him.

"We can never get a moving picture if he's going to run away!" exclaimed Blake.

"They'll stop him soon," said Mr. Hotchkiss. "Come on."

On they ran, and they had not gone far before the lion was brought to bay. Snarling and growling, he stood in the midst of a large circle of the spearmen. Their leader shouted.

"He's calling us to come up with our picture machines," explained the sergeant. "Come on."

The boys ran forward. The lion was not in sight now, but the grinning chief of the hunters pointed to a clump of thorn bushes which moved now and then. And there was no wind to stir them.

"Simba!" exclaimed the chief.

"The lion is there," explained the sergeant. "Put your cameras on that little mound, and you'll have a good view of the whole thing."

Blake and Joe planted their machines, taking different positions, so that if the view of one was obscured the other would have a good chance to get a film.

"Ready!" called the sergeant, and the hunters began closing in. Slowly the circle narrowed. Stealthily the blacks advanced. Joe and Blake took picture after picture. It was a tense moment.

With a terrific roar the lion leaped from his cover and stood in the open, lashing his sides with his tail. The very ground seemed to vibrate with his rumblings.

"I hope he doesn't break through that line and come for us," spoke Blake.

"Same here," echoed Joe, grinding away at his machine.

Nearer and nearer came the warriors. The lion wheeled about seeking an opening. There was none in that circle of bristling spears.

But, seeing a place that the beast evidently thought was weak, he made for it. The chief called out something, and the men braced with their spears, ready for the shock.

"There he goes!" cried Joe. "I can't get a good view! The men are in my way!"

"I'll film it!" shouted Blake.

With a roar the lion leaped into the air, and at one of the men, who rose from a crouching position to receive it. While the beast was yet in midair the black man threw his spear. Like a shaft of light it struck the lion, and passed completely through him, the head appearing on the other side.

In spite of this wound the lion did not falter. On he launched himself, straight at the man, who caught him on his shield. But the lion, reaching over the top, clawed and bit the native on his shoulder. The brave Masai never faltered, however, and began jabbing the lion with another spear passed to him by a fellow hunter.

With shouts the other warriors closed in on either flank of the beast that was bearing down their comrade. Scores of spears flashed in the light. No living creature was proof against them.

"He's done for!" cried Blake, who was busy with the machine.

"And so is the man, I guess," said Joe.

The warrior had been borne to earth, but his shield partly protected him. The lion was now hidden by the blacks surrounding him, and stabbing him with their spears. There came a last rumbling roar, and the fight was over.

With shouts the men dragged the big body, twitching in death, from their comrade. The lion fight was over.

"And, oh! what a film I've got!" cried Blake.

"I got most of it, too," said Joe.

There was much loud talking and ringing laughter among the hunters, while some applied rude but effective treatment to the wounded man. He was not as badly hurt as at first supposed, the ox-hide shield having protected him.

"And they're used to being clawed," explained the sergeant. He talked with the head hunter, who explained that the lion was the very one that had been devastating their village. They recognized him by a spear wound in his flank, given by a native the beast had attacked.

There was further rejoicing among the blacks, as they carried off the body of the lion, as well as the form of their comrade, on their shields, Joe and Blake filming the triumphant march and the dance of rejoicing around the fallen foe.

Then, returning to where they had left their porters, our friends once more started on the trail they hoped would lead to the captive missionaries and Jessie Duncan.

For three days they traveled on, sometimes easily and again under hardships. The trail seemed to become more and more plain as they advanced, and there were indications of foraging and hunting parties having made trips into the jungle.

"We'll soon be up to them," said the sergeant, one afternoon.

"And what will happen?" asked Mr. Duncan.

"It's hard to say," was the answer, "but we must prepare for the worst."

"Or the—best!" exclaimed C. C., in hearty tones.

Just as dusk was settling down they came to the outlying huts of an African village. The expedition closed up, and the porters grasped their spears. The whites got out their guns.

"According to all signs this is where the trail ends," said the sergeant. "We will ask them what we want to know, and if they have the captives here—"

"We'll make them give 'em up!" cried Joe, fiercely.

Nearer they came to the village. Men and women and children ran out. There were excited shouts and cries, and then, to the astonishment of all, the porters began to sing and dance. They rushed forward and clasped hands with the villagers.

"What does that mean?" asked Joe, bewildered.

"They don't seem very hostile," said Blake.

Sergeant Hotchkiss talked rapidly in the native dialect. Then, turning to the whites, he said:

"We've made a mistake. We've been on the wrong trail all the time!"

"The wrong trail?" asked Joe. "Weren't these the natives who were at the burned mission station?"

"Yes, but not until after it was burned. They came from there, and it is their trail we have been following. But the other savages were there before them, and did the damage. We have followed the wrong trail!"

CHAPTER XV
AT THE WATER HOLE

DISAPPOINTMENT WAS THE PORTION of our friends. They had been so sure all along that they were on the right trail that to get to the end and find that all their work had been a failure came as a shock to them.

"Are you sure you are right?" asked Mr. Duncan. "Is it not possible that these natives may be deceiving us? Have they hidden my daughter away somewhere?"

Eagerly he looked through the gathering dusk amid the native huts. Joe, too, started forward, followed by his chum.

"No; I think these natives are honest in what they say," spoke Sergeant Hotchkiss.

"But there is just a chance," said Blake.

"Hardly, when you consider the attitude of our own porters," went on the former soldier. "They are of the same tribe, and have many things in common. There could hardly be a chance to deceive. No, I think we have come on the wrong trail, and will have to start back and begin over again."

It was hard, but there was nothing else to be done. The villagers welcomed their unexpected guests, and set aside some huts for the use of the porters. Of course the whites camped by themselves in their tents. Soon supper was being served and later a walk about the place convinced even Mr. Duncan that he need have nothing to suspect of these Africans.

Their head men told a straight story. They had been off on a hunting trip and had passed through the burned village. They even appropriated some of the things overlooked by the natives who had pillaged it, but this was all.

"Then it means another search," said the father of the captive girl.

"But that will be successful—I'm sure of it," declared C. C. Piper. "We'll find her next time."

"I'm sure I hope so," spoke Blake.

They began their return trip the next morning, refusing an invitation from the friendly natives to stay and take part in a hunt with them.

"We might get some good moving pictures," said Blake. "But I want to get on with our main quest."

"So do I," said Joe.

And so back they went. The advance to the place of the burned village was without incident, save that some moving pictures were obtained of the smaller animals feeding and drinking. Some monkeys were discovered and a very funny film was made from their antics, as Joe, hidden in the dense underbrush, filmed them at their play.

"I think you boys are in for something good," said Mr. Hotchkiss one day when they had gone about a day's journey away from the pillaged mission station, on a new trail this time.

"What is that?" asked Joe.

"At a water hole not far off now," was the answer of the former soldier. "It's the main one for this region and all about it is quite a dry stretch. You ought to be able to get some fine views there if you can secure a good location and remain undiscovered."

They had made a careful inspection of the burned station on again reaching it and, when they had almost given up hope, they had found a very much frightened native boy who had been witness of the original attack. He had attended the mission school a short time, and when the black warriors, in a spirit of wantonness, it would appear, descended on the peaceful station he had run away and hid. Later he came back and for some time had been living in the vicinity. He pointed out a totally different route taken by the pillagers and he stated that they had carried off the white captives.

"Thank the Lord for that!" exclaimed Mr. Duncan. "Then Jessie may yet be alive—she and Mr. and Mrs. Brown."

And so they had taken the new trail—the one they hoped would be the right one.

"A water hole; eh?" said Blake, when he heard about it. "What sort of pictures ought we to film there, sergeant?"

"All kinds," was the answer. "You may get anything from a giraffe to a lion, or from a baboon to a rhino. Water in the jungle makes all wild animals of a kin—for the time being—though later they may fight like cats and dogs."

They traveled on, and it was late that afternoon when Happy One, who, as usual, was in the lead, stopped, threw down his burden and began dancing about, brandishing his spear.

"What's up now?" asked Blake.

"Maybe he sees an elephant or a hippo," suggested Joe, "and he wants C. C. to kill it, so they can have broiled steak for supper."

"I don't believe it's that," remarked Sergeant Hotchkiss, who was riding beside the boys. "I think it's water he sees and we will need it soon, for our canteens are nearly empty. It's been a dry march," which was the truth indeed.

"Then this must be the water hole!" exclaimed Blake.

"I hope it is," said Joe. "I'm as dry as a bone, and the water in my canteen tastes like mud!"

It was the water hole, as they soon saw. Coming up to where Happy One was dancing about and singing, the boys looked down into a sort of level valley, in the centre of which were a number of depressions containing water.

"Water hole!" exclaimed Mr. Piper; "it looks like a whole lot of holes."

"There are a number, fortunately," said the former soldier. "But it is generally spoken of as a 'hole.' There are a number of places where the different animals can drink, though in very dry weather, when there is only one, partly filled, there are terrible fights for the right to the few drops that remain."

"Look!" cried Joe. "What are those small animals running away from the pools?"

"Monkeys and baboons," answered Mr. Hotchkiss. "They generally drink when they can get the chance, for almost every other animal will drive them away. They have to drink when they can, but our coming evidently frightened them. Do you think you can get some pictures here?"

"I'm sure we can," said Blake, as he noted that there were a number of large trees in which their cameras could be placed and screened from view.

"We'll try it tomorrow," said Joe, and so it was agreed.

They went into camp not far from the water hole, but as it was likely that many wild beasts would come to the drinking pools after dark, unusual precautions were taken. The tents of the whites, as well as the primitive sleeping places of the blacks, were surrounded by a thorn bomba, or fence. Large fires were built and guards posted with guns.

It was some time after the night meal before Blake or Joe turned in. They were getting their cameras ready for the morning. Then, too, the strangeness of the surroundings impressed them. And they watched the blacks cooking their primitive meal and preparing to sleep.

But at last the boys turned in, glad that the ticks and mosquitoes were comparatively scarce in this camp.

It must have been after midnight when Blake was suddenly aroused by a peculiar whistling noise. At first he thought he was in New York and that the fire engines were passing. Then he was more fully aroused by a nudge from Joe.

"What's the matter?" asked Blake.

"Something's going on!" cried his chum. "There's a row at the water hole. The sentinels are all excited."

Once more that peculiar whistling grunt sounded.

"Rhinos!" exclaimed Sergeant Hotchkiss from the next tent. "And a fight is on at the pool. Boys, if you had a flashlight you could get a dandy picture now!"

"We've got a long-burning one!" cried Blake. "Let's try it, Joe! Let's try for a night picture."

"I'm with you!" exclaimed his chum, tumbling out, while the excitement at the water hole grew, and there came many cries from the natives.

CHAPTER XVI
A RHINOCEROS CHARGE

"Where's that flash powder, Blake?"

"I don't know. Hand me my shoes, will you?"

"There they are, right by your cot. Don't knock that camera over!"

"Say, you fellows are so excited you don't know whether you're standing on your head or on your heels," complained C. C. Piper, as he looked into the tent, lighted by a swinging lantern. Indeed Joe and Blake were somewhat upset at the prospect of making a new kind of moving picture.

"Oh, we'll get there after a bit," said Blake, as he completed dressing. Joe, too, was soon ready and got out the cameras.

Meanwhile the native porters, learning that they were not expected to get out and assist at a night hunt, had ceased their excited cries. Mr. Duncan took occasion to warn the boys to be careful and then went back to his tent.

"But I suppose I'd better go with you," remarked Mr. Piper, grimly, as he looked to his gun. "There's no telling but what you might try to get too close a view of Mr. Rhino."

"And, if you don't mind, I'll trail along, too," said the sergeant. "I haven't often watched a night scene at a water hole; especially one lighted up."

"I hope our plan works," spoke Joe. "It's a sort of experiment, making a light that will give the brilliancy of a flash, and yet last long enough to get a series of views."

"How did you fix it?" asked Sergeant Hotchkiss.

"Oh, we used some magnesium and other chemicals," explained Blake. "Mr. Hadley told us about it. Are you ready there, Joe?"

"Sure thing."

"Plenty of film in the camera?"

"A thousand feet."

"That ought to be long enough. How about the light?"

"It'll burn for half an hour, I think."

"That's good. Now if the beasts don't get scared when they see the flash, and leave the water hole, we ought to get a dandy film. Come on, I'm ready."

They started from their camp, passing out of the ring of thorn bush used as a fence, making toward the water hole.

"Wow, listen to that!" cried Blake, as a vibrating roar came from the direction of the drinking place.

"A lion, all right," remarked Joe, grimly. "We may get more of a picture than we bargained for."

"And hark to those rhinos," added his chum. "They must be having a great old time."

"A fight, probably," said the sergeant. "They have a very thick skin, but when one rams another, those heavy, sharp horns make terrible wounds."

The noise at the water hole seemed to increase. The roaring of the lion became louder and then died away. It was almost silent for a time.

"The lion has driven everyone else away," explained the former soldier. "He drinks alone. When he leaves the others will come back and finish."

"Then let's get there while the lion is drinking," suggested Blake. "We want to film him."

They hurried on and, a little later, came to the water hole. The moon was just coming up, making a brilliant light, but of course not strong enough for moving pictures.

"I guess this will do," said Blake in a low tone, as he indicated a place where the camera might be set.

"You look after that and I'll 'tend the light," offered Joe.

"And we'll stand by the guns," suggested Mr. Piper.

Thus it was arranged. They could see shadowy forms moving about near the water hole, but could not make out what animals they were.

"Light up!" called Blake, when he had the camera set.

"Light she is!" exclaimed Joe, and a moment later the scene was brilliantly illuminated. A strange picture was presented as Blake began to turn the handle of the camera.

Somewhat back from the water hole were a number of baboons, sitting on their haunches, seeming to grin in their ugly fashion at some other animal. Some of the ape-like creatures were chattering angrily. Then came a growl, and the boys noticed a big lion slaking his thirst at the pool.

"Old Mr. Leo drove the baboons away," whispered Blake.

"That's right," answered his chum. Their low voices did not disturb the lion, but the light did. Startled, the king of beasts looked up to see the cause of the flare. The baboons did also, but none of them ran away, as the boys feared would be the case.

"Maybe they think it's moonlight," suggested Joe.

"Queer moonlight," remarked Blake; "but as long as they think so, it's all the better for us," and he continued to grind away at the machine. The slight clicking noise seemed to bother the lion at first, but, looking carefully about, and seeing nothing and, as the wind was blowing from him to the boys and he did not scent them, he seemed to conclude that everything was all right and went on drinking. Nor were the apes or baboons suspicious after the first few minutes.

The lion finished drinking and walked slowly away, the camera registering every movement. Then the baboons, with shrill chatterings, came rushing back to the water.

"Some pictures, these," remarked Blake.

"I should guess yes," agreed his chum.

The scene was ever changing. The baboons rushed away in a body and a herd of some small deer came to the pool. Then a slinking leopard drove these timid creatures away. In his turn the fierce cat gave way to a troop of howling hyenas. Though these scavengers of the jungle singly, or even in pairs, would never dare to molest a leopard, a body of them will become so bold that they will sometimes even attack a lion—and kill it, too.

Yard after yard of the film was reeled off, making a series of rare pictures. As yet the position of the boys had not been discovered, for they were well screened and only occasionally did some beasts hear the clicking of the camera and look suspiciously in that direction.

"I guess we won't have to use the guns after all," remarked Mr. Piper.

"It doesn't look so," agreed the sergeant.

They had hardly spoken, however, before there came that same peculiar, whistling grunt that before had attracted their attention to the water hole.

"Rhinos!" exclaimed the sergeant, getting his rifle in readiness.

From the underbrush, at the far side of the hole, a big body emerged, and a moment later a huge rhinoceros stepped into the glare of the light. The calcium seemed to frighten it for a moment, and then, concluding that, as no one was in sight, everything must be all right, the great beast came on.

It had hardly begun to drink, however, before there was another of the queer grunts, and a second rhinoceros rushed out toward the water. The second one did not seem to see the first one until almost at its side, and then the first one, raising its head, noticed the other.

With lowered heads, the two great horns on each one prominent, they stood for a moment motionless, and the sergeant whispered:

"They're going to fight!"

The words were scarcely out of his mouth before there was a rush and the two came together with an impact that could be heard for some distance. The magnesium light made everything almost as clear as day, and Blake kept on taking pictures.

The fight did not last long. The first rhinoceros, with a quick, savage motion, thrust its horn into the other's side, inflicting a grievous wound. The injured animal, with a grunt of pain and dismay, backed off, and, after standing motionless a moment, turned and walked slowly off, staggering.

"He's badly hurt," whispered Blake.

"I should say so," agreed his chum. "He can't last long. But what pictures we're getting!"

The victorious rhinoceros walked back to the pool, seemingly satisfied. Blake was getting a series of pictures, somewhat different now, for in the background were several waterbucks coming on to the pool. Suddenly the film in the camera broke.

"Pshaw!" exclaimed Blake aloud, before he thought. "Now we'll lose some good scenes while I fix that."

"We ought to have brought two cameras," said Joe.

"Quiet!" hissed the sergeant. "He'll hear you."

But it was too late. The big rhinoceros had heard the sound, and though the eyesight of this animal is the poorest of all jungle beasts, save the elephant, its scent and hearing are most acute. The creature had heard the boys talk and had sensed from whence it came.

With an angry, whistling grunt he rushed straight for the place of concealment, gathering speed as he came.

"We'd better run!" cried Joe.

"Save the camera, whatever you do!" exclaimed Blake.

"He's going to charge!" shouted the sergeant. "Get your gun ready, C. C.!"

While Joe and Blake folded up the camera tripod and shifted it to one side the two men, with ready rifles, stepped out where they would have a clear range to shoot. The rhinoceros was now close enough so that he could make out his enemies in the strong light.

"We've got to stop him!" cried the former soldier.

"Here goes!" came from Mr. Piper, as he leveled his gun.

"I'm with you," echoed the sergeant, as he got into a position to blaze away at the infuriated beast.

CHAPTER XVII
THE ELEPHANT TRAIL

THEY BOTH FIRED TOGETHER, taking the best aim they could under the circumstances, for it is not the easiest thing in the world to hit a rhinoceros in that fashion, nor to strike a vulnerable spot.

"Again!" cried the sergeant, as he threw out the empty shell, and injected a loaded one into the firing chamber. "That won't stop him!"

"Here goes!" exclaimed C. C. Piper, grimly.

Together they fired again and this time they could see the great beast waver in his charge.

"Keep on going, boys!" cried the soldier to Blake and Joe, who were making the best time possible out of danger, with the camera containing the precious films held between them.

"He's a tough one!" shouted C. C. "I'm afraid we'd better run for it ourselves, sergeant."

"Not much! We'll stop him yet!"

Although it has taken some little time to tell this, it did not actually take more than a few seconds to happen. On came the lumbering beast, but the fusillade of shots was too much for it. Bullet after bullet snapped out from the two heavy rifles, and, though it might seem like cruelty, they were not shooting for sport, but to save their lives.

Then, when he had almost reached the two intrepid men who stood there facing him, the rhinoceros stumbled and came to his knees.

"We've got him now!" sang out C. C.

"One more shot to finish him!" cried his companion.

And, as the creature was endeavoring to rise, a final bullet sent it over dead.

"That was a narrow squeak!" said Joe, as he and Blake came to a stop.

"That's right, old man. But, oh! if only the film hadn't broken, and we could have had a picture of that charge."

"It would have been great," agreed Joe, "but we may get another chance for one."

"Not like that one," sighed Blake in disappointed tones. "But I suppose we ought to be glad that we got off so luckily."

"Indeed you had," spoke the sergeant. "A charge by an angry rhino is nothing to laugh at."

"Are you going to take any more pictures?" asked C. C. as Mr. Duncan, accompanied by a number of the native porters, came running from camp to see what the firing meant.

"No, I guess we have enough," said Blake, "It will take a little time to join the broken ends of the film, and I guess the light is about burned out."

"That's right," said Joe, and, as he went to see how much longer it would last, it flickered out. So they gave up picture-taking for that night, well satisfied, however, with what they had. In the moonlight they made their way back to their tents and to sleep, though most of the porters, hearing of the slain rhinoceros, stayed up to get some meat. Then they lighted big fires and had a feast that lasted until nearly morning.

When daylight came, Blake and Joe found the reason for the breaking of the film was that some of the mechanism of the camera was out of order. They decided to stay in camp until it could be repaired, and perhaps this was a wise move, for the porters had eaten so much meat that they could hardly walk.

There was no need to kill any more game for the table, and thus every one had a rest except Joe and Blake, who busied themselves about their picture machine.

The next day it rained and, as they did not know what sort of trail they might meet deeper in the jungle, they decided to remain where they were until it cleared. But it continued to rain for two days and they spent them drearily enough, there being little to do. Mr. Duncan fretted because they were not making progress toward finding his daughter, but there was no help for it.

Then came clear weather, and with Happy One to lead the now well-satisfied porters the expedition again started off. They were in a good game country now, and while for some time afterward the boys did not get a chance to make any extraordinary pictures, still they got some. And there was plenty to eat, which kept the porters in good humor.

For nearly a week they traveled on, sure now that they were on the right road, for they made inquiries at small native villages through which they passed, and learned that the party of raiding Africans had gone through on their way back into the interior.

"But did they have white people with them?" cried Mr. Duncan, after a native chief, through an interpreter, had been asked about the raiding party.

"Him say yes!" replied Happy One, who spoke several dialects. "One white man and two missies!"

"Oh, that must be Jessie and her friends!" cried the father of the missing girl.

Sometimes they received wrong information, not intentionally given, however; and occasionally no amount of questioning could bring out any facts about the white captives.

Either the natives in the villages, where they made the inquiries, had not observed carefully enough, or their scouts, or cattle-watchers, who were naturally the ones to have observed the raiding party on its way back, had been too timid to get close enough to learn the real facts.

"But, on the whole," decided Joe, when they had talked the matter over, "I think we're on the right road."

The others agreed with him, and so they kept on.

It was not easy traveling. Most of the way lay through a dense jungle, with only a narrow native trail, which necessitated going in single file. Occasionally they would cross a plain, and this was always welcome. Once they had to ford a river.

Then came a time when Blake came down with a touch of jungle fever and they had to stay a week in one camp to nurse him. But he recovered, and once more they were under way.

One afternoon, after fairly cutting their way through a tangled growth of jungle vines, in order to shorten the trail a bit and get to one that a native chief had told them about, Joe, who was in advance, came to what seemed like a road cut through the forest.

"It looks as if we were coming to something!" he cried. "This looks good to me. Let's take this path, even if it is longer."

Sergeant Hotchkiss came running up. Taking one look at the swath through the jungle he cried out:

"Boys, it's an elephant trail, and a big, fresh one, too! We'll follow that and, if you have luck, you'll get some rare pictures. Hustle up, everybody!"

CHAPTER XVIII
SOME RARE PICTURES

HAPPY ONE SENT BACK the call to the porters in the rear, and at the news of elephants there were mingled expressions. While some of the black men chanted of the power of the mighty beast, seemingly somewhat afraid of it, others declaimed of the sure-shooting abilities of the white men, and improvised chants concerning the amount of meat they would soon have to feast upon.

"And there sure is some meat on an elephant," said the former soldier. "I hope we don't have to kill any; but, if we do, there'll be a feast such as you never saw before."

"Is elephant meat good to eat?" asked Joe.

"The natives will eat almost anything," said the sergeant, "as long as it's meat. But, of course, there are some parts of an elephant better than another. The heart is as good eating as I ever enjoyed, and the trunk makes fine soup. Elephant's feet, properly cooked, are delicious."

"Elephant's feet!" cried Blake. "I've eaten pig's trotters, but elephant's—"

"The way to do it," said the former soldier, "is to make a hole in the ground, build a fire in it, get a lot of hot embers ready, and bury the foot in them. Go off for the day, and when you come back the meat inside the foot will be roasted to a turn and no beef or mutton can equal it. But we may not get an elephant."

"We'll make a hard try for some pictures, anyhow," said Blake. "Let's get our cameras ready, Joe."

"Oh, you've got plenty of time," said the sergeant. "Though this trail is comparatively fresh, still a herd of elephants can travel much faster than you would think, merely to look at them. They are a good many miles off now, and, though they may stop to feed, we can hardly come up to them today. It may take three days."

"But it's a good trail to follow," spoke Joe.

"Yes, indeed," agreed C. C. Piper. "When a herd of elephants go along, they don't stop for small obstacles. They knock down anything that gets in their way. That makes it good for us. But if we go after these big beasts we may all—"

Unconsciously he was falling into his old habit of predicting misfortune, but he caught himself in time, as he saw Blake and Joe looking curiously at him.

"You didn't catch me that time!" he cried, gaily. "Everything is going to be lovely, and you'll get some fine views; I'm sure."

"That's the way to talk!" cried Blake, encouragingly.

"Well, let's move," suggested Joe. "This is better than crawling through a jungle."

"But won't it take us too far away from our search?" asked Mr. Duncan, anxiously. "I want to get to the village where those desperate kidnappers are. My poor Jessie may be suffering all sorts of hardships."

"I appreciate that," said the sergeant, gently; "and we won't lose a moment more of time than is necessary. But we must keep the porters well supplied with meat, or they will desert us, and then we would be helpless in the midst of the jungle. So if we can get an elephant it will be to our advantage.

"Then, too, this trail is an easy one to follow, and though it is somewhat out of our way we can, in the end, save time by following it."

"That's all I want to know," said the father. "I want the boys to get their pictures; but, oh! I do so want to find Jessie!"

"And so do I, Dad!" cried Joe. "And we will find her, too. We won't waste any time, but we've got to depend on our porters when it comes to the last, and there may be a fight."

"Yes, that is so," admitted Mr. Duncan.

They took up the elephant trail, and followed it until nightfall. They made camp near a spring, and Joe, who went out to trace a bird with a peculiar call, was lucky enough to shoot an eland, which furnished the camp with meat, and sent the porters into transports of joy.

Early the next morning, after an uneventful night, save that lions roared in the distance, and hyenas howled, they again took up the trail. They followed it for three days, but could not seem to come up to the big creatures. Once or twice they heard them in the distance, crashing through the underbrush, and pulling up thorn trees on which they fed. But the wind was blowing from behind, carrying the scent from the hunters directly to the pachyderms, so that they were continually being alarmed and kept on the march.

"But when the wind dies down, or changes, we'll have a good chance," said the sergeant, and C. C. Piper agreed with him. "They'll get tired of being continually on the move," went on the former soldier, "and stop to rest."

"Maybe they'll lie down and go to sleep," suggested Joe.

"Elephants sleep standing up, as a rule," said the sergeant. "It's only one of their queer habits."

But if the boys did not get elephant pictures as soon as they hoped, they did get some other rare films. Once they were lucky enough to snap a herd of zebras, and again a number of wild ostriches were come upon. The latter were nearly the cause of a tragedy, for, after the pictures had been taken, one of the porters, not understanding what was going on, came from where the other blacks had made a temporary camp, and started across the plain where the big birds were.

A cock ostrich chased him, and as the kick of these birds is as bad as one from a horse, with the additional danger that the toe-nails can cut like a knife, the black man was in peril. He started to run, but the ostrich was speeding after him.

Happy One saw his fellow porter's danger and called out something in their queer tongue.

"What is he saying?" asked Blake, while C. C. caught up his gun and drew a bead on the angry bird.

"He is telling him," translated the sergeant, "to pick up a piece of thorn bush, and hold it in front of the bird."

"What good will that do; charm it?" asked Blake.

"No, but there is a very tender spot in the neck of an ostrich, just under the head," said the sergeant, "and it dreads the prick of a thorn there more than anything else. That's the only way to protect yourself from one of the big birds."

The black man did as directed. As he ran he caught up a long piece of thorn bush. Turning, he faced the ostrich, and, as he advanced the thorns toward the bird's neck, the creature stopped and then began to "waltz" around the porter, seeking an opening. But the man continually presented the thorn bush at the creature, and then, getting a good chance, C. C. shot the big bird.

"Too bad," said the actor-hunter; "but it had to be done." Blake and Joe had filmed the odd scene, and later they took some of the ostrich feathers as souvenirs, some of the porters adding the plumes to their already fantastic headdresses.

"I wonder when we will come up to those elephants?" asked Blake a little later that day, when they were once more on the march.

"The trail is getting fresher," said C. C. "We ought to be up to them soon."

"I'll have one of the porters climb a tree, and see if he can make them out," said the sergeant.

The black man had scarcely reached the top of a tall bamboo standing on the edge of the broad trail, than he set up a shout.

"What does he say?" demanded Blake.

"He sees the elephants!" cried the sergeant. "Get ready now, boys. The wind is in our favor, and you may be able to get some pictures of them feeding."

CHAPTER XIX
A SHOT IN TIME

CAUTIOUSLY THE MOVING PICTURE boys made their way along the elephant trail. They had two cameras with them, for they remembered the accident that had interfered with their getting a film of the charge of the rhinoceros, when the celluloid broke at a critical moment.

"Though I don't know that I care for an elephant charge," said Blake, grimly. "A rhino is bad enough, but an elephant is about three times as big, and so must be three times as bad when he comes after you."

"More than three times as bad," declared Sergeant Hotchkiss; "especially if it's a rogue elephant."

"What kind is that?" asked Joe.

"It's a solitary elephant, who, for some reason or other, likes to flock by himself," explained the former soldier. "He gets unreasoning fits of rage, if elephants ever do reason, and runs amuck, just like some of the Malay natives. He'll charge a stone wall, if he takes a notion, and once he gets after a hunter it's all up with the man unless he can make a kill or reach shelter. But I don't imagine there'll be any in this herd. As I said, they usually go about by themselves."

The natives of the expedition had been left behind, so as to render the noise of the advance less loud, and the only ones in the party were the whites, the two boys, Mr. Duncan, C. C. and the sergeant. The three latter carried guns, while the two lads had all they could manage with their cameras.

"We will only shoot one, unless there is danger," said the former soldier; "as that will give us meat enough."

Carefully they advanced, until presently they could hear the noise made by the big beasts as they fed, pulling off branches of the trees, breaking small trunks and limbs under their ponderous feet, or with their trunks.

"There they are!" suddenly whispered the sergeant, as he motioned to the others to come to a halt. He pointed through an opening in the trees, and there they all saw the herd feeding in a little glade, up to the edge of which the jungle trees came.

"Now if we can only get some pictures!" said Blake.

"We'd better climb a tree," suggested Joe. "Then we can get a better view."

"There's a good one over there," suggested C. C.

"I'll take that," spoke Joe, "and, Blake, you can get in the one next to me. We'll work one camera, but if anything happens to that we'll have the other in reserve."

So it was arranged, and soon the two lads were making their way up into the trees, moving as cautiously as possible. There were low branches which made the ascent comparatively easy, and they carried with them light but strong cords, by which their cameras could be hoisted up. They could not use the tripods, but hoped, by resting the machines on a limb, to make them steady enough.

"Oh, this is a fine view!" cautiously called Blake to his chum, it being agreed that Blake was to make the first try for the pictures.

"Yes, and I have a good one, too. If you break a film or anything else happens, I can go right on from where you leave off," answered Joe.

The elephants, a score or more, totally unconscious of the nearness of their deadly foe—man—were contentedly feeding. In this case they need have nothing to fear, for the hunting party of our friends was not organized for needless slaughter. One beast for food was what they had limited themselves to.

It was a curious sight, and as Blake reeled off the film he could not but feel glad that he had the opportunity of seeing the huge beasts in their native wild. Some were feeding, and others were rubbing themselves against trees to scratch their thick hides, often infected with ticks or other jungle parasites.

They ate in a peculiar manner. Reaching up with their trunks they would pull off big branches. Holding to one end of these they would put the foliage of the branch in their mouths and pull it out as one would a bunch of currants, thus stripping off the tender leaves, which they munched contentedly, casting aside the now useless branch.

Blake was making picture after picture, getting some rare ones. The wind continued to blow from the elephants to the boys, bringing with it a strong animal odor, but preventing the huge beasts from scenting their watchers. On the ground below stood C. C. Piper, Mr. Hotchkiss and Mr. Duncan, with their guns ready for any emergency. They were going to try for a shot at the beasts when the films were completed.

"I guess I've got enough," said Blake. "I'll get down now. The elephants are getting uneasy and it seems as if they were going to start off again."

"Go ahead," suggested Joe. "I'll stay for a while and maybe I can get something different."

Blake had lowered his camera to the ground and was about to descend himself, when, a short distance down, he slipped and fell with a crash. He was stunned for the moment, though not much hurt; but he made considerable noise.

Instantly the herd of elephants became aware of danger. The leader, a big bull, trumpeted shrilly and the others gathered together ready for a rush into the jungle.

"Get that view, Joe!" called Blake, as he staggered to his feet. As he did so he became aware of a sharp pain in his right ankle. He could not walk.

At that instant the big bull, hearing the lad's voice, became aware of the location of his foes. Raising his trunk high and with open mouth, his big tusks standing out, the huge fellow rushed straight at Blake.

"Shoot! Shoot!" cried Mr. Duncan, who was so nervous that he realized it would be useless for him to try.

"Both together!" said Sergeant Hotchkiss, in a low voice to Mr. Piper. "We've got to stop him short!"

They aimed quickly. On came the elephant, trumpeting with rage, while the others in the herd joined in. They all began to move toward Blake, who was hopping away as fast as he could on one foot, having abandoned his camera. Joe was still in his tree, but could easily be shaken out of it.

"Ready!" cried the sergeant. "Fire!"

The two guns were discharged as one. The elephant was almost up to Blake, crashing through the bushes. But the men had fired straight, true, and just in time.

The heavy bullets halted the elephant long enough for the lad to make good his escape. Crashing to its knees the big beast tried to rise.

"Give him another!" yelled the former soldier, and again they shot together. The elephant crashed over on its side. Blake had been saved in the nick of time. The other elephants, shrilly trumpeting, made off in the jungle and Blake's camera, with its rare film, was rescued from the bushes where it had dropped.

CHAPTER XX
DOWN THE RIVER

"WELL, SHALL WE CHANCE it?" asked Sergeant Hotchkiss, as he stood on the bank of a jungle river.

"It seems to be the only thing to do," spoke Mr. Duncan. "Our information is to the effect that the native camp we wish to reach is down in this direction, and the river offers the best route."

"Except that we haven't any boats," put in Joe.

"But we can make a raft," suggested his chum.

"And that's what we'll have to do," said C. C. Piper; "though it may capsize—no it won't either!" he cried, with a sudden change of feeling. "A raft will be just the thing!"

This was several days after making the pictures of the elephants feeding, when the shot in time had prevented the big bull from taking vengeance on Blake. The latter's ankle, sprained when he toppled out of the tree, was almost well again, though it had necessitated a stay in camp of two days, and for two days after that the lad was carried in a sort of litter by some of the porters.

The slain elephant had a pair of magnificent tusks and they were taken along as trophies. As for the meat, nothing in that line came amiss to the Africans, and there was a feast that lasted for several days.

The boys had their first taste of elephant trunk soup, roasted heart and the delicacy the sergeant had told them about—elephant's foot. Joe and Blake voted it very good.

Then had come a period of traveling through the jungle, during which they had suffered much. The insect pests were very troublesome, ticks and mosquitoes abounding. Then one of the porters was bitten by a snake of a poisonous variety, but fortunately not so virulent that the man died. He was far from well, however.

The weather had been bad and one rainy night followed another, the thunder and lightning being terrifying. Then, too, one of the porters was mauled by a leopard that sprang out of a tree on him as he was going to the spring for water. The big cat was shot by Blake, but the man suffered very much and was incapable of any hard work.

Then they had come to the banks of a fairly large river down which, according to native information, was an African village that might be the home of the kidnappers.

"Well, it seems to be the only thing to do—to try a trip down it," said Mr. Hotchkiss, when they had held a consultation about it. "River travel is certainly easier than on land, in a jungle, and we'll have to cross it sooner or later, for I have a general idea now where the country lies that we are trying to reach."

"But how are we going to go down the river when we have no boats?" asked C. C. Piper. "We can't swim—and I've had enough of that anyhow, since leaving the California coast."

"We can get the natives to build a big raft," suggested Mr. Hotchkiss. "On that we can float down, but we can't very well take the animals," for they still had with them their riding mules and those that carried packs. Several of the animals had died from the bite of the tse-tse fly, but as the expedition was constantly using up food and supplies, the burdens of the dead animals were transferred to the heads of the porters.

"What can we do with the animals?" asked Mr. Duncan.

"Leave them back at the village we passed a little while ago," suggested the former soldier, and this was agreed to.

Happy One declared that his men could soon build a raft that would carry them all, but when it came to the making of it the whites found it better to superintend the details themselves.

"They'd have it come apart in the middle of the river the way they were binding the logs together with vines," said the sergeant as he made the blacks correct some of their faults. "We want it substantially made."

But when the rafts were about done (for they decided to make two) they were ample for all. The animals were to be left behind, and, with the packs and bundles, the moving picture cameras and films, those already exposed and new ones, the start down the river was to be made some morning soon.

While the raft-building was going on Joe and Blake had some opportunity to go out into the jungle, near the river camp, and make moving pictures. Though they got no remarkable ones they did succeed in filming a rhinoceros upon whose back were a number of tick birds.

These curious feathered creatures are to the rhinoceros what the pilot fish are to the shark. They warn of danger. The big-horned animals of Africa, in common with most of the mammals, are infested with ticks, an insect that lives by sucking the blood of the beasts. Tick birds feed on these ticks and often perch on the backs of the rhinoceroses and pick them off.

But the birds are very shy and easily made aware of danger, not only to themselves but to their animal feeding-ground. They fly off at the first alarm, and as soon as they go the rhinoceros knows that he must look out for himself. Once the tick birds fly from his back he begins to use the natural faculties most useful to him.

Blake and Joe were getting some fine pictures of a rhino feeding, and as the wind was right, the beast did not scent them. Presently, however, the tick birds became aware of something unusual going on.

CHAPTER XXI
THE LONE MESSENGER

"LOOK OUT!" EXCLAIMED BLAKE, as he saw the bird sentinels fly from the back of the big beast.

"What is it?" asked Joe, who was working the camera.

"He'll be coming this way soon if he happens to see us. He's getting uneasy now that the birds are gone."

Joe, who had been looking at the mechanism of the moving picture machine, glanced over toward the rhino. The huge creature did indeed seem to be getting restless.

He stopped feeding and began sniffing the air, at the same time peering about with his little pig-like eyes. The birds were circling about, seemingly in an endeavor to locate the enemy they had sensed. Whether or not they would locate them our heroes did not know. They were fairly well screened amid some bushes, but this would offer no barrier to the rush of the rhinoceros.

With the birds gone the rhino knew something was wrong and it began casting about to discover it, either by the sense of smell or his sharp hearing. But the wind carried from him to the boys, consequently he did not get their odor, nor did the slight clicking of the machine carry to him.

With a puzzled "woof" and his peculiar whistling grunt the big beast finally moved off into the depths of the jungle, crashing his way through the underbrush. The tick birds followed as if satisfied that their walking restaurant had done the right thing.

"There he goes," said Blake, with a sigh of relief, for they had brought no guns with them and were some distance from the river camp.

"Yes, we got some good pictures and without any danger," observed Joe. "Well, shall we get back?"

"Might as well, I guess," agreed his chum, and they took to the trail again, a deserted elephant path through the fastness of the jungle affording good footing.

On their way back they had rather a curious experience. They had often read of the honey bird, but had not yet seen one, and when a little feathered creature began circling about them, uttering a peculiar note and seeming to be urging them to follow, Joe said:

"That must be a honey bird, Blake."

"I believe it is. Let's trace it and see if we can pick out a honey tree. Maybe that story about it is all bosh."

But it was not, as they soon found. The bird flew on ahead of them, perching in one tree after another until it had led them about half a mile. Then, alighting on the limb of a gum tree, it stayed there, calling shrilly.

"The bees must be near here," observed Joe. They looked around and, finally attracted by the buzzing of some insects, they located the bees' nest in a hollow tree.

Building a fire, which they caused to smoke heavily by piling damp leaves on it, they had soon routed most of the bees, and then with a small hatchet they had with them they managed to chop out a portion of good wild honey, some of which they took back to camp with them.

"And where does the honey bird come in?" asked Joe.

"There he is now, eating the bees and grubs," said Blake, pointing to the wise little creature which had been joined by others like it. They were having a great feast, and indeed it seems that the bird does lead men to the nest of bees in order that it may get what otherwise it could not—a share of the sweet stuff and the succulent larvæ.

The honey formed a welcome addition to their meal. The rafts were completed now, and the next day the expedition started down the river, the pack animals having been left behind.

The trip down the stream was interesting. There was not so much life to be seen as there was in the jungle, but there were any number of crocodiles—big ones that seemed at first to be mere floating logs, but which soon came to life when the raft passed. A number of pictures were made of the unprepossessing saurians and, once or twice, great hippopotami came so close that it seemed they were going to attack the rafts. But the big boats were too solid to cause any fear in regard to them, and Joe and Blake filmed the huge creatures as they swam alongside, often with their mouths open to their widest extent.

The progress was not fast, but it was much easier than traveling through the jungle. There were no bundles to carry, and the blacks seemed to appreciate this.

All day long they stretched out on the rafts, improvising their queer chants and songs, now poleing the craft out from the shore when the current carried them too far in, or keeping out from rapids they might run upon.

At times a halt would be made to enable game to be shot, for it was necessary to keep the party in meat, and it all had to be killed fresh in that equatorial climate.

They had been four days going down the river and were beginning to wonder when they would come near the location of the kidnapping natives. Mr. Duncan was beginning to get more and more worried as he approached what he hoped would prove to be the place where his daughter was held captive.

"Oh, if Jessie is only alive and unharmed!" he exclaimed, "everything else will be all right."

"Of course she'll be," declared C. C. Piper, who had only once or twice relapsed into his former gloomy moods. "Of course she'll be all right and we'll soon find her."

"We'll have to send out a scouting party soon," declared Sergeant Hotchkiss.

"Why?" Joe wanted to know.

"Because we don't want to come upon that native camp unexpectedly. We don't want to rush into danger. There may be a big crowd of 'em and if we can take 'em unawares we'll have so much the better chance to rout 'em. Yes, we must soon send out a scouting party."

"Can Joe and I go?" asked Blake, eagerly.

"Hum! Well, I suppose so," was the former soldier's answer. "But we'll need some native guides, too."

They had moored the rafts to the river bank that evening, for they did not want to chance running down the stream in the dark, and were just making a camp when Blake, who was looking across the water, called out:

"Here comes the biggest crocodile I've seen yet. Get a gun, C. C., and have a pop at him. Maybe we could take the skin home for a souvenir."

They all looked to where he pointed. In the gathering dusk they could see some object coming up stream. It did seem larger and higher out of the water than crocodiles usually swim. The motion, too, was different.

"Crocodile!" cried Sergeant Hotchkiss, when he had taken a glimpse of it. "That's no crocodile."

"What is it, then?" asked Blake, curiously.

"A native in a dugout canoe," was the answer. "It's a solitary native and it's strange, too, seeing him all alone."

"He's seen us and he's going to turn back," put in Joe.

Then Happy One, the leader of the blacks, called out something in his native tongue. There was a moment of silence and back floated an answer across the stream.

"What does he say?" asked Mr. Duncan.

"Happy One assured him that we were friends," translated the sergeant; "and asked who he was and where he was going."

"What did he say?"

"He said he was a messenger going for help for some captives."

"Help for some captives!" cried Blake. "Maybe he can tell us something about those we are after!"

Sergeant Hotchkiss started in surprise, and then shouted something to Happy One, who immediately set up a great shouting. The lone messenger in the canoe, that was hollowed out of a solid tree trunk, hesitated a moment and then waved his paddle.

CHAPTER XXII
AN AFRICAN CAMP

"HERE HE COMES!" CRIED Joe.

"And he doesn't quite know whether he's going to be captured, or whether we're friends," remarked Blake. "Joe, do you s'pose it's possible that he can be from—from your sister and her friends?"

"I don't know. It sounds too good to be true. Don't let Dad hear you say that, or he may be terribly disappointed if it turns out wrong."

The lone messenger was paddling his clumsy boat toward the raft.

"We'll soon know what's up," remarked Mr. Piper. "That is, if he can speak any ordinary language."

"Oh, I guess between our natives and the sergeant we can make out," spoke Blake.

The messenger came on more slowly, as though the nearer he approached the more timid he became. They could see him plainly now—a big, tall native with rather more clothes than his kind usually wore. He carried in the boat with him a keen-edged spear and a big club that seemed to have been often used.

A little way from the shore he halted his boat by sticking his paddle down in the muddy bottom and then he called out something. Happy One answered and the two carried on quite a conversation, with Sergeant Hotchkiss occasionally putting in a word.

"What's it all about?" called Mr. Duncan, impatiently. "Has he any news for us—good news?"

"The very best we could expect!" exclaimed the sergeant. "It appears he is a messenger—one of those captured from the mission station and carried off by the raiders along with the whites."

"My daughter!" cried Mr. Duncan. "Is she alive—was she one of those carried off? Oh, tell me quickly!"

"I'd better tell you the whole story as I heard it," said the former soldier. "Happy One, tell him to come to the camp and eat. He must be half starved."

And from the manner in which the messenger ate it would seem that this was so.

"He was one of the natives living in the mission settlement," explained the sergeant to those gathered about him in that portion of the camp set aside for the use of the whites. "He was one of the Christian natives and everything was going well, when this party of Africans, who belong to one of the worst tribes of the whole continent, came along and made the raid, burning the place and carrying off all whom they did not kill."

"And—and my daughter—Jessie?" exclaimed Mr. Duncan.

"She and Mr. and Mrs. Brown were carried off, together with some men, women and children of the natives," said Mr. Hotchkiss. "They were intended for slaves. After many hardships the captives were brought into the village where their captors lived. There they were treated meanly, but none of them was killed.

"Finally the whites managed to get word to this young man, urging him to try to escape and take word of their plight to friendly natives, asking to be rescued.

"Chako, for that is his name, watched his chance and did succeed in getting away. He got a spear and a club and managed to sneak off in this boat. A week ago he started to paddle up stream. He was afraid to move, except at night, and his progress was slow. Once he was thrown overboard by a hippo ramming his craft, and again a crocodile nearly got him. But he kept on, and when he saw us he had just started out on his night trip. He did not know whether or not to trust us, but when he heard the friendly words of Happy One he decided to appeal to us."

"And he comes from Jessie?" asked Joe.

"Yes, she is one of the white captives, though Mr. and Mrs. Brown were the ones who directly sent the message."

"How—how is she?" faltered Mr. Duncan. "How is Jessie?"

"Unhappy and much frightened, as you may suppose," said the sergeant; "but she was in no immediate danger when Chako left."

"How far is it to their camp?" demanded C. C. Piper, as he looked at his elephant gun.

"About two full days' journey down the river, and then one day into the jungle."

"Then let's start at once!" cried Jessie's father. "I must get to my daughter."

"It will be better to wait until morning," suggested the former soldier. "It isn't altogether safe to travel at night; and then, too, we can make better time by daylight."

"Oh, and to think that this native has lately seen my little girl, whom I have not beheld in so long!" exclaimed the father. "Ask him how she was—tell me all about her!"

"He doesn't know much," replied the sergeant. "The whites were separated from the black captives, so he had little chance to speak to her. But we ought to—oh, well, we'll start at once, as soon as it is daylight," said the sergeant, suddenly interrupting himself. "I'll tell Happy One to have the natives in readiness for a quick start. And—well, I guess that's all," he concluded as he walked over to where the messenger was being entertained by the porters.

Blake followed. There was something in the manner of Mr. Hotchkiss that worried him. When he got a chance to speak alone to the former soldier the lad asked:

"Is there anything wrong, Mr. Hotchkiss? Is there more need for haste than you told?"

The man looked around and, seeing neither Joe nor his father near, said:

"There is, Blake, grave need of haste, but I didn't dare speak before them. It seems that within a week these kidnapping natives are to celebrate one of their most cruel feasts. Many sacrifices are to be made and it may be that in their frenzy they may injure the whites. Though up to this time they have been rather in awe of them, for they know the far-reaching power of the British government.

"But when they are mad with their religious rites there is no telling what they may do. Yes, there is need of haste. I am going to tell Mr. Piper what I know, and with his help and yours, while keeping Joe and his father in ignorance of the imminent danger, we will make as much speed as we can without seeming to do so."

"A week off; eh?" mused Blake. "That ought to give us plenty of time."

"Yes, but we don't know what delays we may meet in the jungle," said the sergeant. "Then, too, this Chako may not have correctly estimated the time it takes. We shall have to prepare for the unexpected. They may proceed with their rites before the week is out. We must hasten."

"That's right," agreed Blake.

They made an early start next morning, the curious boat Chako had paddled in being put on board one of the rafts.

Fortune favored them, for they soon came to a part of the river where the current was swift, and they made good time. The members of the expedition had caught the fever and were anxious to hasten on to try conclusions with their black enemies.

Spears and shields were looked to. Some of the natives improvised bows and arrows and a few had blow guns. Our white friends overhauled their weapons and ammunition.

"I hope it doesn't come to a fight," said Blake. "But if it does—"

"We want to be prepared," finished Mr. Hotchkiss.

The boys had no chance now to take moving pictures, even had they been in the mood. All their thoughts were centered on the rescue.

Finally the day came when Chako, the lone messenger, indicated that they were to leave the river and strike inland. The rafts were moored to the bank, though it was doubtful if they would be used again, for it would be almost impossible to pole them up stream.

Into the jungle they struck, with Chako in the lead as a guide. This part of the journey he had correctly estimated and at dusk one day he signaled for a halt.

"What is it?" asked Mr. Duncan.

"The African camp, or village, that he escaped from," said the sergeant. "We are here at last!"

CHAPTER XXIII
THE ATTACK

THEY WERE IN A dense part of the jungle. On all sides of them were immense trees, growing so close together that one could see only a little way in either direction. Between the trees grew a great tangle of vines and pendant moss, making an almost impassable barrier, save to an elephant or buffalo.

They had followed a rude trail, that, at times, was almost lost sight of. But Chako seemed to know the road by which he had escaped, and led on unerringly. Occasionally they would come to a swamp in which there was danger of sinking to one's hips. But now they were near to the place where they hoped to rescue the captives.

"What's to be done?" asked Blake, as they came to a halt in the midst of the now almost twilight darkness in the dense jungle.

"Rush right in and rescue my daughter and her friends!" cried Mr. Duncan.

He actually started forward, catching up one of the guns carried by a native bearer.

"Hold on! That won't do!" cried the sergeant. "We must map out a plan of campaign. To rush in now would be the worst kind of folly. They would either overwhelm us, for they far outnumber us, or it would bring about the very thing we are trying to avoid—"

"You mean they might—might do something to the captives?" asked Blake.

"That's it," the sergeant went on. "We've got to use strategy in this attack. And one of the first things we've got to do is to get to some place where we can camp without the noise penetrating to the village. Then we can make our plans."

Chako indicated that the African camp was still some little distance in advance, but added the information that scouts from it might be anywhere in the jungle, and might discover the presence of the rescuers and give the alarm.

"Then back we go," decided the sergeant. "We'll camp at the last spring we passed and have supper. Lucky we've got the fresh meat we killed this noon, or the natives would go hungry." For on the march that day C. C. had managed to kill a big antelope for food.

They feasted—at least the natives did, for they could eat no matter what impended—but the whites were too anxious to enjoy the meal. No unnecessary noise was made, for, though they were some distance from the village, there was no way of telling when black scouts might be about.

"I think a night attack will be best," said the sergeant, when it had all been talked over. "That will take them most by surprise and give them the least chance of harming those we have come to save."

"Do you mean attack tonight?" asked Blake;

"No, it is too late to do that now. I suggest that we rest tonight and tomorrow try to see how the situation is. Then we can attack with some chance of victory. Chako can probably tell us which side to make the advance against. And then—"

"By jove! I have it!" suddenly cried Joe. "The very thing for a night attack."

"What?" asked Blake.

"Fireworks!" went on his chum. "You know we have quite a box of them that we got in Entebbe, expecting to use them in trading with some of the native chiefs, but we haven't even opened them. They're still in the water-tight package. Now what's the matter with using them in the attack?"

"The very thing!" exclaimed the sergeant. "Couldn't be better. We'll attack tomorrow night. Now to get some rest and when it's daylight we'll see if we can spy out the camp."

With Chako to lead them, Sergeant Hotchkiss, Blake and Joe made a cautious advance on the village early the next day. Mr. Duncan and C. C. Piper were left behind to stand guard, for there was no telling when a party of the kidnappers might take a notion to penetrate the jungle.

Approaching cautiously, the two moving picture boys and the sergeant, guided by the messenger, soon came within sight of the native village. It was a typical one, with the thatched mud huts—many of them—arranged in some sort of order. One large hut, in the middle of the village, seemed to be that of one of the chief men, and Chako whispered that it was there the king dwelt.

"And what are those smaller huts near his—the huts where the men stand in front with spears?" Mr. Hotchkiss wanted to know.

"The white captives are there," was the answer. "The young girl and Missis Brown and her man."

"My sister there!" exclaimed Joe, with sparkling eyes. "Oh, I hope I can soon see her."

"Patience," counseled the sergeant. "Now to plot out the best method of advance." They were looking down on the village from a little hill to the north of it. The native town lay in a clearing in the jungle that surrounded it on all sides.

"I don't see any better way of making the attack than from here," said Mr. Hotchkiss, after a pause. "It is easy to reach from our camp, too."

"Then we'll attack from here?" asked Blake.

"One party will. The other will circle around and execute a flank movement. We'll have them between two fires, and I guess that will take them by surprise. It may be possible to rout them without any serious loss. I hope so, for I don't want to take lives—not even of these savages."

"I think the fireworks will do the work," declared Joe.

The scouts returned to the camp and the plans were talked over and finally decided on. The attack was to be made just before daybreak, as Chako said the Africans always slept the heaviest then, and even the sentinels would probably be dozing after their hearty meal of meat.

So it was arranged. The night passed slowly—all too slowly for the anxiously waiting ones. Then the sergeant gave the order to advance. There was a late moon, which gave enough light for them to see their way, as silently they approached to the attack.

It was no easy task, marching through the jungle to make the attack. Hard enough it would have been in daylight, but with blackness all around them, hardly able to see where they were going, it was difficult in the extreme.

"I do hope we make out all right," murmured Blake, who was marching near Joe.

"So do I, old chum. It's a slim chance, but we've got to take it. If only we can surprise the beggars before they rouse up enough to know what hit 'em, we'll have it easier."

"Yes, I suppose so. That's the worst of it, though. They are so used to awakening at the slightest sound that they may rouse up before we get ready to attack 'em."

"We'll have to take our chance, that's all."

"Silence back there!" suddenly called Mr. Hotchkiss, as the murmur of the boys' voices reached him. "Don't talk any more than you have to."

For a time they marched on silently, the only sound being the crackle of dried reeds as they broke under foot, or the occasional swish of the branches of trees under which they passed.

"And to think that your sister is off here in this wilderness," whispered Blake, when they had gone on a little farther. "This is a small world, after all."

"It is," agreed Joe. "To think that, only a comparatively short time ago, you and I were farm-boys. Now we're in the African jungle and we don't know what will happen."

"That's right," remarked Blake. "But if your sister is safe so far, there's no reason why we shouldn't rescue her. I think the idea of the fireworks is a dandy one."

"Yes, if they only go off," spoke Joe.

"Why shouldn't they go off?"

"Oh, it's so wet here. Land! when you get up in the morning your shoes are so damp you can hardly get them on. And as for your clothes, you might just as well sleep in a Turkish bath."

"It is damp," agreed Blake.

"And if the fuses don't light easily we'll be out of it," went on his chum. "You see the plan is to surprise them, and the fireworks will do that, if they shoot off quick enough."

The march continued, until suddenly, from the van, there came a cry of alarm. It seemed to come from one of the natives.

"What's that?" exclaimed Blake.

"Quiet up there!" commanded Mr. Hotchkiss.

A low, gurgling cry succeeded the scream of alarm, and Mr. Hotchkiss ran up ahead. Joe and Blake could hear him questioning.

"What is it? What has happened? Is anyone hurt?"

There was a jangle of sounds as the Africans rapidly explained something. The marching column halted, and those in the rear fretted over the delay. Presently Mr. Hotchkiss came back.

"What is it?" asked Mr. Duncan.

"One of the porters bitten by a snake," was the answer.

"A snake!" cried Blake.

"Well, that's what he *thought* it was," said Mr. Hotchkiss. "It really was only a big thorn he stepped on, though. But he might have raised the whole jungle about our ears if he hadn't been quieted."

"What did you do for him?" asked Blake.

"I handed him an old key-ring I happened to have in my pocket," said Mr. Hotchkiss. "It had some keys on it, and he was tickled almost to pieces with the jingle. He forgot all about his hurt, and quieted down. I just had to have silence. It's ticklish business at best, sneaking up on an African camp."

"Are we near there?" asked Joe.

"Yes, pretty close now. Don't make any more noise than you can help."

Again the line was formed, and the advance continued. It went on in silence for some time, until suddenly, off to the left, there came a sound like distant thunder.

"What's that?" asked Joe.

"Lions, I guess," replied Blake.

From the natives about them came the murmur:

"Simba! Simba!"

"Quiet there!" commanded Mr. Hotchkiss. "No lions will come near this party. Move on!"

The roaring died away, only to be repeated a little later, somewhat farther in advance.

"This is bad," murmured Blake.

"It sure is," agreed his chum. "If those beasts make an attack it's bound to give the whole game away."

"Oh, what a picture this would make!" murmured Blake.

"But we wouldn't dare try to film it," said Joe. "It would give us dead away. Hark to that, would you!"

As he spoke the very ground seemed to vibrate with the sound of the roaring of the lions. There was almost a panic of fear among the natives until the white men in charge had assured them that there was no danger.

A halt was made, and a number of the black men begged that fires might be lighted to scare away the jungle beasts. But Mr. Hotchkiss knew this would be risky. Instead, he ordered those of his companions who had them to display their pocket electric torches. These tiny, flashing lights seemed to have the desired effect, for the roaring of the lions died away.

Then the cavalcade advanced once more, Joe's mind filled with anxious thoughts about the rescue of his sister.

The natives carried their spears, or bows and arrows. The white men had their guns, Joe and Blake had a revolver each for use in emergency; but their main arms were the fireworks, carried for them by several bearers. On reaching the mound where they had spied on the camp that afternoon a party, under C. C. Piper, was sent around to begin hostilities in the rear.

"Fire as soon as you are there," said Mr. Hotchkiss. "But shoot in the air. If we can scare them, without hurting any one, so much the better. Ready now! March! As soon as you attack, we'll get busy here!"

CHAPTER XXIV
A VICTORY

WAITING IN THE DARKNESS, looking down on the camp of the kidnapping Africans, Joe, Blake and the sergeant, and the blacks with them, listened for the echoes of the shots that would tell of the beginning of the attack. C. C. Piper and Mr. Duncan, with about half of the porters and Chako, were in the second party.

"I wonder what will happen," asked Blake, "when the firing begins?"

"There'll be one grand rush," said Joe, "and it will be up to us to make it a worse one. The more we can demoralize them the better it will be for us."

"That's right," agreed the sergeant. "Get 'em wild, so they don't know what's happening, and we can rush in there and make our rescues. I hope we shall be able to save some of the missionaries' friends as well as your sister and Mr. and Mrs. Brown, Joe."

"I hope so, too. Lucky we got here before they began their so-called religious ceremonies—these kidnappers."

"That's right. Chako said they might start tomorrow, though. We're only just in time."

"And it will soon be tomorrow," spoke Blake, softly. "It will be daylight in a short time."

They looked down on the camp. Here and there a sentinel fire could be seen burning dimly, but even the guards had gone to sleep, it seemed, for none could be observed pacing about. It was as the messenger had said—they all slept heavily toward morning.

"They ought to be there by this time," said the sergeant after a long pause. "I wonder if anything could have happened to—"

He was interrupted by several shots that echoed through the night. The darkness, over on the far side of the camp, was cut by several jagged splinters of flame.

"There they go!" cried Blake.

"Now for the fireworks!" sang out his chum.

Once more came a burst of rifle fire from the other attacking party.

"Let 'em go!" shouted the sergeant.

The scene was now one of confusion. The blacks in their camp, sudden-ly awakened by the volleys, were rushing about, yelling at the top of their voices. They could not imagine what was going on. A few shots came in return—shots from old-fashioned muskets that did no harm.

Then, with a mighty roar, a big skyrocket shot over the African camp, scat-tering fire and sparks and colored balls in its train. It was followed by several others; Roman candles, and then several other forms of pyrotechnics, set off by Blake and Joe, shot through the darkness.

The effect was startling. The blacks who had started to run away from the rifle fire, harmless as it was, for the shots were directed into the air, were met by the rain of sparks from the aerial bombs and other pieces of Fourth of July ordnance the moving picture boys touched off. There was considerable noise, too, for some of the pieces burst with loud reports.

"How are you making out, Joe?" called Blake from the place where he had stationed himself—a sort of clearing behind a clump of mimosa trees.

"Fine and dandy. How about you?"

"Oh, I'm all right. I've set off a lot of those big skyrockets. Say, they're peaches! Did you see how they burst?"

"I should say yes! One nearly went off before I was ready for it—too short a fuse. I got ready to run."

"That's right. Here goes for one of those bombs! I'm glad we had these things with us."

"So am I!"

For a time the chums could not speak to each other, though but a short distance apart, for the noise of the fireworks was almost deafening. The jungle was lighted up with the hues of many-colored fires, and the wild beasts were thrown into a panic by the unusual demonstration.

There sounded the deep-voiced defiance of distant lions, which died away to be replaced by the shrill laughing-like sound of hyenas that were always hanging about, slinking around to see if they could not make a meal off what some stronger or more brave beast had killed.

Then would come the chatter of monkeys disturbed at their slumbers, or the scolding of parrots or other birds of the dense forest. It was as though the morning sun had unexpectedly risen and called into life all the inhabitants of the jungle.

Mr. Duncan came running up to where Joe and Blake were stationed, and, in the glare of a bursting rocket, they saw that his face was blackened with powder.

"Have you seen her, Joe?" he gasped. "Did you get a sight of her?"

"No, Dad," replied the brother of the girl they had come so far to rescue.

"Did you, Blake?"

"No, Mr. Duncan. But it's so dark, and we aren't quite near enough to the camp yet. We'll get her all right, never fear."

"Oh, boys, I can't help being worried. It means so much to me. Think how I would feel if those natives—those Africans—should turn against her at this last minute and—"

Mr. Duncan was so affected that he could not go on.

"Now, Dad, you don't want to think anything like that!" exclaimed Blake, heartily. "We'll scare these fellows so they won't know where they're at. Come on here! Help Blake and me set off some of these fireworks. We've got more than we can handle!" and he thrust into his father's hand a torch used to ignite the fuses.

"That's the way to talk to him!" said Blake, in a low voice. "Keep him occupied. Then he won't think so much about your sister. I think she's safe—don't you, Joe?"

"I hope so."

"Oh, she must be. Why, it was all quiet when we stole up, and we've been so busy ever since that they haven't had time to rush off with her to another part of the jungle. They must think this is a shower of meteors, or something like that."

"I hope they do," murmured Joe, as he brought up another rocket from the box where the supply was kept.

The shooting of the pyrotechnics was kept up for some time longer. Then C. C. Piper, who had been industriously letting off bombs and Roman candles, seemed to beat his own energetic record. For there was a great burst of fire from where he had stationed himself, and then his voice was heard to call:

"Help! Come here! I'm getting shot!"

"What is it?" yelled Joe.

"Come here and you'll see! I guess I must have—" his voice was drowned out in a burst of noise that sounded like the letting off of strings of firecrackers.

Guided by the glare and brightness, Joe and Blake rushed through the jungle to where their old friend had stationed himself. As they reached him they saw him rushing about in the midst of a lot of sparks, while all about him balls from Roman candles shot in various directions.

"What is it? What is it?" cried Blake.

"I dropped a match in a box of fireworks!" yelled Mr. Piper. "They're going off!"

"I should say so," agreed Joe.

As he spoke a skyrocket that must have been lying on the ground, or some flat surface, shot over his head with a whiz and a roar.

"Look out!" yelled Blake. But he need not have spoken, for Joe ducked instinctively and the rocket, colliding with a tree, burst with a loud report and a shower of fire.

Then came another, so close to C. C. that the actor's clothes were set ablaze.

"Gee whiz!" cried Joe. "This is the limit!"

"Help! Help!" cried Mr. Piper, vainly endeavoring to beat out the flames.

Blake, seeing the danger, ran to a pool of water, and filling his hat, dashed the liquid over the man. The spray served to put out the flames, and Mr. Piper, beating out the last remaining sparks with his hands, tossed some damp earth on the smouldering box of fireworks.

"That's over, anyhow!" he remarked with a sigh of relief.

"Come on!" yelled Joe. "One last volley and I think we'll have 'em on the run!"

Then the native porters set up shouts of triumph. They were answered with wild yells of fear from the kidnappers. The shooting redoubled in its sound and glare.

"Give 'em all we have!" yelled Blake, as by the flare of the rockets he saw the mass of natives huddled in the centre of the village, too terrified to move.

"All we have—that's right!" echoed Joe, as he sent another aerial bomb aloft. "It's now or never."

The fusillade was greeted with a chorus of groans and yells. Then there burst out a blaze from the centre of the village.

"One of the huts is on fire!" cried Blake. "The sparks have caught on the thatched roof!"

"And it's the king's, too!" yelled Joe. "Come on, or the other huts may catch—the ones where Jessie and the missionaries are. Come on!"

"Go ahead!" cried Sergeant Hotchkiss. "I guess we've got 'em on the run!"

And so they had. Endeavoring to escape from the fire of the guns on the south, the Africans had rushed to the north, there to be met with the fusillade of skyrockets and Roman candles. It was too much for their superstitious natures. They might stand a human assault, but the fire from heaven was too much.

With howls of fear they rushed off to one side—off into the jungle, deserting their village. Men, women and children fled, leaving their captives to those who had come to rescue them. It was a complete victory.

"Come on, Dad!" shouted Joe, as he and Blake rushed into the deserted native village, several huts of which were now ablaze. "We'll get Jessie!"

"Jessie! Jessie! Where are you?" cried the anxious father. "We have come to save you!"

CHAPTER XXV
SISTER JESSIE

FOR A MOMENT THERE was a lull in the noise. The firing had ceased, the skyrockets and Roman candles had died away. The aerial bombs no longer crashed like thunder overhead.

The attacking party, flushed with victory, ceased for the time their cries of delight at the ease with which they had driven off their enemies.

As for the kidnapping natives, they were no longer in sight, for they had slunk off into the jungle, fearing the just vengeance of those whom they had despoiled and captured.

"Jessie! Jessie!" shouted Mr. Duncan again. "Are you here? We have come to save you."

There was silence again, and then from one of the smaller huts, near the one where the king had dwelt, came girlish tones.

"Who is calling me? Yes, I am here. Oh, Mr. Brown, is that you? What has happened? Where is Mrs. Brown? Oh, what is going on?"

"Jessie! Jessie!" called another voice—one that seemed to come from an adjoining hut. "I did not call. I don't know what to make of it. My wife is here, but she has fainted. I can't get out. I'm tied. So is she. Can you escape and tell me what it is? I fear the village is on fire. I heard guns—"

"So did I. Oh! if it is only a rescue—" her voice faltered and she could be heard to sob.

"It is a rescue!" shouted Joe. "Dad and I have come for you, Jessie. I'm your brother. Father is here!"

"Father—brother!" faltered the tones. "I have none. I am all alone—"

"Hurry out before the hut catches fire!" cried Mr. Duncan, who, in rushing toward the rude building, had stumbled and fallen.

"I am a prisoner—tied fast," the girl's voice answered. "Oh! whoever you are, save us!"

"Come on," yelled Blake. "This whole place will be on fire in a few minutes. We've got to get 'em out!"

They dashed for the huts. It was a matter of seconds only to tear aside the grass cloth that served as doors. Then the flames from several burning huts lighted up the interior.

Joe, leaping inside the one whence the girl's voice had come, saw tied to the centre pole a maiden. With his knife he slashed the bonds of twisted fibre and, catching her in his arms as she fell forward, he cried:

"Jessie! Jessie! I've found you at last. Here she is, Dad!"

Mr. Duncan rushed in. Taking the burden from Joe he carried the girl out of the hut, the roof of which had already caught. In the light of the fire he looked at her pale face.

"Yes, it is Jessie—my Jessie!" he exclaimed as he kissed her. "Though I have not seen her since she was a baby I would know her anywhere. Oh, Jessie, we have you again! I have my son and daughter now!"

The girl opened her eyes. Wonderingly she looked at Joe and his father.

"Is it—is it really true?" she faltered.

"It is!" Joe assured her. "Blake, come over here and let me introduce you to Sister Jessie."

"Say, this is no time for introductions!" cried C. C. Piper, breaking in on the happy little party. "This is a fierce fire. We've got to rescue those missionaries and skip. This whole place will go!"

"Oh, yes, dear Mr. and Mrs. Brown!" cried Jessie. "We must save them."

"It's all right. I got them out," said Sergeant Hotchkiss. "They were tied to the centre pole of their hut, but here they are all safe. Not harmed a bit," and he stood to one side to disclose those whom he had rescued.

"Oh, Jessie! can it be true that we are saved?" cried a lady, as she rushed up and clasped the girl in her arms. "I had almost given up hope."

"The Lord is very good to us," said a man's voice behind her, and then Mr. Brown went on: "Dear friends, we cannot thank you enough. It is all a mystery to me. I do not even know you, but can it be possible that our dear little missionary helper has found the relatives she suspected she had, but about whom she was never sure—can she have found them in this strange fashion?"

"No, we found her!" cried Joe, laughing. "But it's all the same!"

"Come, hurry away from here!" cried C. C. Piper. "It's getting too hot. We can talk later."

"That's right," agreed Mr. Brown.

"What about the native prisoners?" asked Mr. Duncan. "We should save them, too."

"They are not confined in any huts," said Mr. Brown. "They were treated as slaves, but not tied up. I fancy they escaped when you drove the others off by your shots. Oh, it seems too good to be true!"

A hasty investigation showed no captives in the huts that were not yet afire, and had there been any in the blazing ones they would have made the fact known by their yells. The rescuing party now withdrew to a safe place, and took possession of some huts that were in no danger of catching fire, as the wind blew away from them.

It was light enough to see to make a camp now, the first flush of dawn coming in the east. The porters, with shouts of joy, took possession of the property of the scattered kidnappers. There was plenty of food, without going back to the camp of our friends in the jungle, and soon everyone was fairly comfortable.

As daylight grew there came straggling back some of the Christianized natives who were captured at the time the missionary workers were, and they were made welcome. But none of the kidnappers came back.

The story of the raid on the mission station was well enough known not to need repeating, and then Jessie told how she had come to take up with missionary work.

She had always wondered about herself since a small child, and had made some effort to trace her parentage, without result. Finally she had been, in a sense, adopted by Mr. and Mrs. Brown and had traveled with them extensively, acting as a helper in their missionary work and eventually coming to Africa.

Of the horrors of the raid and the terrors of their trip through the jungle and as captives little was said. They wanted to forget it. Jessie told how, in a moment amid the mad scenes, she had written the message in the Bible and tossed it out, hoping some friend would find it.

"And it will be easy to forget all the sad scenes now that I have a father and a brother," said Jessie, as she looked at them both fondly.

"Our trip ended most successfully," said Blake. "Not only did we get some of the best moving pictures ever filmed, but we found what we came after—Sister Jessie."

"And what will you do next?" the rescued girl wanted to know, when they had related their strange adventures since coming to Africa, and had told of their work in filming many weird scenes.

"It's hard to say," replied Joe. "Things seem to come our way most unexpectedly." But what they did next and what happened to them will be told of in the next book of this series, to be called "The Movie Boys in Earthquake Land"; or "Filming Pictures Amid Strange Perils."

After a rest in the partially burned African village the expedition was reformed and with the former captives—white as well as black—the start for Entebbe was made. There were hardships on the way, but they put up with them as best they could. The boys got several more fine films of wild animals, some secured with no little danger, and they shot some big game.

"I wouldn't have missed this for the world," said Blake when they were on the steamer on the way to New York, accompanied by C. C. Piper, Mr. Duncan, Jessie, of course, and Mr. and Mrs. Brown. For the missionaries decided to take a vacation, as Mrs. Brown was very nervous because of her captivity.

"It sure was great," declared Joe. "I hope our circus man likes the films."

And that he did need not be doubted, for Blake and Joe were by this time experts in the moving picture business. And thus, safely on their way to New York, we will take leave of our heroes and their friends.

www.ingramcontent.com/pod-product-compliance
Lightning Source LLC
Chambersburg PA
CBHW011437170626
46808CB00009B/3090